Helen

Helen

BY

TRACY WILSON

http://beautifulpublications.com

Published by
Beautiful Publications LLC
Stratford, CT 06614

This book is a work of fiction. Names, characters, places, and incidents are either products of the author's imagination or are used fictitiously. Any resemblance to actual events or locales or persons, living or dead, is entirely coincidental.

PRINT ISBN: 978-1-7362753-6-8
EBOOK ISBN: 978-1-7362753-7-5

Printed in the United States of America

Disclaimer

This is fiction. This is **NOT** a true story. My mother-in-law was kind, compassionate, and soft-spoken. I never had any problems with her. The woman I'm writing about is someone else's nightmare – not mine.

Introduction

I don't know why I bothered. I could've walked away from the both of them – but I chose not to – don't ask me why. Was the dick good? Oh yea – it was good – but I was no where near dickmatized – until it was too late. I tried to be a good daughter-in-law to someone that never had any intention of being my mother-in-law - or anybody else's mother-in-law for that matter. Her only intent was to drive a wedge between me and her son so she could maintain her position. She had to work harder than most when it came to me because I was pushing her out of the top spot before he got the pussy – and she knew it. She also knew she would be irrelevant soon enough – I made it clear to her by my actions that I didn't want her anywhere near us – and I damn sure wasn't going to give her grandchildren! You're probably wondering why I didn't just give her a chance – well let me tell you – I gave her plenty – and she made my life a living hell! It finally got to a point where I decided to take control of my life and my sanity – and now that I look back on everything – I've realized that if I had checked her myself instead of waiting for him to check her, she might still be alive...

"Hey..." he called out, trying to get my attention. That was an instant turn off. I ignored him and kept walking towards the door... "Excuse me..." he said as he pulled my arm...

"Let go of me!" I snapped as I yanked my arm away from him...

"I'm sorry..." he said as he let go of my arm... "I was calling you and you didn't hear me..."

"Was that you saying hey?"

"So you did hear me..." he laughed...

"If you wanted my attention, the better way would have been to say excuse me miss – If I heard that I probably would've turned around..." I said in an annoyed tone...

"Excuse me..." he said as he picked up my hand and then kissed it... "Miss..." I couldn't help but smile... "You have a nice smile..."

"Thank you..."

"May I buy you a drink?"

"Not tonight – I'm tired – I need to get home..." I answered as I went to open the door to leave and he blocked me...

"May I buy you a drink tomorrow night?"

"It depends on how I feel when tomorrow gets here..." I sighed...

"How 'bout this – I'll give you my number – if you feel like having a drink – call me..."

"Okay..." I sighed...

"Look – if you don't really want my number..."

"Stop playin' and give me your number!" I laughed...

"Give me your phone..." I took my phone out my pocket and handed it to him. I watched him put his number in and then he handed it back to me. I smiled when I saw his name...

"Harland..." I read as I smiled. He smiled back at me as I put my phone back in my pocket...

"May I have your name?"

"I'll give it to you when I call you..." I answered as I started to open the door and he blocked me again. Before I could say anything he spoke...

"Let me get that..." he said as he opened the door...

"Thank you..." I said as I went outside and he came out behind me...

"You're welcome – you need a ride?"

"I'm getting an uber..."

"You mind if I wait until your uber gets here?"

"I don't mind..." I answered as I took my phone out my pocket and order the uber... "Five minutes – thank God!"

"Rough day?"

"Not rough – just long..." I sighed...

"Is this your uber?"

"Yes – thanks for waiting..."

"You're welcome..." he breathed as he pulled me into a kiss. As much as I liked it, I pushed him away from me...

"I'm sorry..."

"No you're not..." I said as I rolled my eyes, opened the door, and got in...

"Lindley Street?" the driver asked...

"Yes..."

"Okay Maam..." the driver said as he drove off...

As soon as I got in the door I called Snow...

"Hey Harmony..."

"Girl – let me tell you!" I exclaimed as I sat down in a huff...

"What happened?"

"I stopped at Park City Bar and Grill for a drink – I had a long day..."

"Okay..."

"So I have my drink – I get up to leave – somebody starts calling me talkin' 'bout hey!"

"Hey? Where they do that at?"

"Exactly – so I kept walkin' – why did this man come up to me and pull my arm talkin' 'bout excuse me – I was calling you..."

"Oh hell no! What?!"

"I snatched my arm away and told him let go of me!"

"I know that's right – da fuck?"

"He apologized..."

"He needed to!"

"He said he was trying to get my attention so I told him a better way would've been to say excuse me miss – if he did that I would've turned around!"

"Exactly!"

"Girl – this man took my hand, said excuse me miss, and kissed it!"

"Aww shit!"

"I know!"

"What happened after that?"

"He asked me could he buy me a drink..." I sighed...

"Why didn't he ask you that before you left?"

"I was thinking the same thing – but I told him no – I'm tired – I need to get home..."

"So you left?"

"No – he asked me if he could buy me a drink tomorrow and I told him it depends on how I feel when tomorrow gets here..."

"Damn Harmony – that's cold!" she laughed...

"I didn't mean it like that!" I laughed...

"Shit – did he give up?"

"Nope – he said how 'bout this – I'll give you my number and you call me when you feel like having a drink – and I said okay..."

"Okay! That's what I'm talkin' about!"

"The way I said it he was like – look – if you don't really want my number – so I said stop playin' and give me your damn number!" I laughed...

"Can you blame him?"

"I know – I gave him my phone and he put his number it it..."

"Bout damn time! What's his name?"

"Harland..."

"I like that!"

"Me too..."

"So you gonna call him?"

"I was... but..."

"Harmony – c'mon!"

"I told him I was getting an uber and he wanted to wait with me so I said okay..."

"What's wrong with that?"

"Nothing..."

"What happened?"

"When the uber came, I thought he was going to open the door for me but he didn't..."

"I know got damned well you ain't mad 'cause he wouldn't open the door!"

"He kissed me..."

"Oh..."

"Yea..."

"Did you like it?"

"Yea..."

"Well what's the problem?"

"It was the way he did it..."

"Oh so he kinda forced it?"

"He pulled me to him and kissed me in the mouth..."

"What?! Oh hell no – I thought he kissed you on the cheek!"

"I pushed him away from me..."

"I would'a cursed him out!"

"He said he was sorry..."

"He wasn't sorry!"

"I know – that's what I said..."

"You need to delete his number – he might be some type of stalker – did he follow you?"

"No..."

"Does he know your name?"

"No..."

"So wait – he doesn't even know your name – and he kissed you?"

"Yea..."

"How's he gonna know who you are when you call him – if you call him – are you gonna call him?"

"I was thinking about it..."

"Did he force you to kiss him like you didn't have a choice or did he just kiss you like – did he take you by surprise?"

"It was more like he wanted to take me by surprise..."

"I dunno Harmony... I think you should be careful..."

"I'm gonna call him..."

"You are?"

"Yea..."

"Oookkkkaaayyy..."

"I'll call you right back..." I said and then I hung up and looked at my phone... "Fuck it..." I sighed as I dialed his number...

"This is Harland – leave a message..."

"Hi Harland – this is Harmony – I just wanted to let you know I made it home..."

"So you think she's the one?"

"I think so..."

"You know she has to go through me first...."

"Yes Mother..." Harland sighed...

"I'm serious – she needs to understand I'm always going to be in your life..."

"I wouldn't have it any other way..."

"So what's her name?"

"I don't know..."

"Is she pretty?"

"No – she's butt ugly!" he laughed...

"Harland!"

"Why does that even matter?"

"Because I don't want no ugly grandchildren..."

"Ma!"

"I don't – we don't do ugly over hear – if she's ugly and she's got strong genes..."

"Ma... stop it... I can't!" he laughed...

"Well if you like her she's probably pretty – you don't know her name so something attracted you to her..."

"Her lips..."

"Her lips? What about the rest of her?"

"That too..."

"So you were attracted to her by her lips? What was she doing with them?"

"Ma!"

"Well – you started it!" Helen laughed...

"I can't explain it – all I can tell you is I had to kiss her..."

"You had to kiss her? Harland – what the hell did you do?"

"I put my number in her phone... I waited with her until the uber came... and when she went to get in... I pulled her close to me... and I kissed her..."

"What did she do?"

"She pushed me away from her..."

"She didn't slap you?"

"Nope..."

"Hmmm – I would 'a slapped you..."

"I know..."

"So you kissed her, she pushed you away from her – and?"

"I told her I was sorry..."

"You'sa lie – you weren't sorry!" Helen laughed...

"That's what she said..." he laughed...

"Wait, wait, wait – you kissed her – she pushed you away from her – you told her you were sorry – she told you you're not sorry – and then she left?"

"Yea..."

"She likes you..."

"I know..."

"Le'me go – I'll call you back later..."

"Love you Ma..."

"I love you too..." she said as she hung up...

"What's this?" he asked as his eyes lit up and he pressed play...

"Hi Harland – this is Harmony – I just wanted you to know I made it home..."

"I love it..." he sighed as he dialed my number...

"Hey Harland..."

"Hey Harmony..."

"I guess you know I'm home..."

"Yes I know... I was just returning your call..."

"That's not all you're doing..." I laughed...

"I wanted to apologize..."

"You're not sorry you kissed me..."

"I'm not apologizing for kissing you... I'm apologizing for offending you..."

"Thank you – I appreciate that..."

"So you were offended?"

"I was taken aback..."

"I'm sorry – I hope I can still buy you a drink..."

"I'll call you..."

"Okay..."

"Good night..."

"Good night..." I sighed as I hung up and called Snow back...

"Hey Harmony – what's up?"

"I left him a message..."

"Okay..."

"He called me back..."

"Aww shit – you sound all happery..."

"I am..."

"I'm glad you're happy... I still think you should be careful though..."

"He apologized again..."

"He's not sorry he kissed you!"

"He apologized for offending me..."

"Oh – okay..."

"I told him I appreciate that..."

"Okay – he gets a point for that – so are you gonna let him buy you a drink?"

"I sure am – I'ma need a drink after I eat!" I laughed...

"I know that's right!" she laughed...

"Hey!" Harland exclaimed as he answered...

"Can you hear me?"

"Barely – where are you?"

"I'm on the train!"

"Where?"

"South Norwalk!"

"What time will you be in Bridgeport?"

"Six o'clock!"

"You thirsty?"

"Thirsty and hungry!"

"I gotchu – I'll see you at 6!"

"Okay!" I yelled as I hung up...

"Good thing you didn't have to yell..." the lady next to me laughed...

"Ha, ha – you funny!" I said sarcastically. I was so glad she got off in South Norwalk. I moved over in the seat, put my music on, turned on my blue tooth, and looked out the window as I began to relax. I jumped when the conductor yelled...

"Bridgeport next!" Good thing he yelled or I would've slept through to Stratford...

"May I sit?" the young lady asked...

"I'm getting out at Bridgeport – you can sit inside if you want..." I answered as I got up so she could slide in...

"Thank you..."

"You're welcome – good night..." I said as I got off the train and headed for the elevator...

"Hey..." Harland breathed when he saw me...

"Hey..." I breathed as I went up to him and hugged him...

"Oh – okay!" he exclaimed as he hugged me back...

"I'm sorry..."

"No you're not!" he laughed...

"I didn't mean it like that – I'm just happy to get off that train..."

"Whatever you say..." he said as he rolled his eyes...

"I'm happy to see you too – is that better?"

"Much better..." he answered as he wrapped his arm around me and led me across the street...

"Where are we going?"

"We're going back to where we started..."

"Okay – we better hurry up then..." I said as I started walking faster...

"Excuse me... Miss?"

"Yes Harland?' I answered as I turned around to face him...

"What's your hurry?"

"Happy Hour is over at 7 – and I really want those appetizers..." I answered as I turned around and hurried towards the hotel with Harland right behind me...

"Are you in such a hurry that you won't let me get the door for you?"

"Get the door!" I laughed...

"Get it yourself!" he laughed...

"Fine!" I laughed as I snatched the door open and we went inside...

"Welcome to Park City – table for one?" the hostess asked...

"Table for two..." I answered as Harland came up behind me...

"Harland – over here!" I heard her say...

"C'mon..." he said as he pulled me towards her table... "Hi – this is Harmony – Harmony, this is my Mother, Helen..."

"Hello Helen – it's nice to meet you..." I said as I sat down. I was fuckin' pissed!

"Can I start you off with something to drink?" the waitress asked...

"Yes!" Helen and I said in unison...

"What can I get you?"

"I'll have a pomegranate martini..."I answered...

"I'll have a margarita..." Helen answered...

"I'll have a Guinness..." Harland answered...

"Are you ready to order?"

"Just bring us one of each of the appetizers..." I answered...

"Don't you think you should let her ask us what we want?" Helen asked...

"Oh – I'm sorry – I didn't realize you'd be here and I told Harland I really wanted the appetizers..."

"It's okay – bring the appetizers..." Harland said...

"Harland – you know those sliders have pork on them – and you also know I don't eat pork!" I felt bad for Harland. I was mad – but I still felt bad...

"You can bring us the sliders without bacon – that's fine..." I said...

"Thank you Harmony..." Helen said...

"You're welcome..."

"I'll go place your order – and then I'll go get your drinks..." the waitress said as she walked away...

"How was your day?" Helen asked...

"Long..." I laughed...

"I was talking to Harland..." I swear to God I wanted to check her – I should've – but she was his mother...

"It was good Mom – Harmony – how was your day?"

"As I said – it was long..." I sighed. Helen was getting ready to say something but the waitress brought our drinks... "Thank you Lord!" I exclaimed as she put them on the table...

"Your food will be out in a minute..." she said and then she walked away...

"To Happy Hour..." I said as I raised my glass...

"I'm not drinking until the food gets here..." Helen said...

"To Happy Hour..." Harland said as he raised his beer and clinked his bottle to my glass. When Harland went to take a sip of his beer Helen stopped him...

"Harland – I really think you should wait until you eat..."

"I think you can take a toast with me..." I said as I picked up the bottle and handed it to him. Harland looked at me, looked at Helen, and I watched her nostrils flare as we both took a sip...

"Here's your appetizers..." the waitress said as she put them on the table...

"Everything looks so good!" I exclaimed as I started taking food off the plates with my fork...

"Harland – aren't you eating?" Helen asked...

"I gotchu..." I said as I put my plate in front of him and took his empty plate. Helen picked up her fork and started to take some of the appetizers and she got irritated when I started to take some too...

“Excuse me – do you mind?”

“Don’t worry – I’ll leave you some...” I said as I continued to fill my plate...

“You could’ve waited until I was finished...”

“We’re splitting everything that’s left – I didn’t think you’d mind...”

“Well I do...”

“Sorry...” I said as I shrugged my shoulders, picked up my drink, and gulped it down. The look on Helen’s face was priceless...

“I guess you were thirsty!” Harland laughed...

“I was!” I laughed – but the real reason I gulped down my drink was because I was ready to go off on his mother...

“How’s everything?” the waitress asked...

“I’d like another one...” I answered as I held up my empty glass...

“Anybody else?” she asked...

“We haven’t had a chance to drink yet!” Helen snapped...

“I’ll have another Guinness...” Harland answered as he held up his empty bottle...

“Harland! You’re driving!” Helen exclaimed...

“Mom – relax – I’ll be fine...” he said as we started eating. Helen shook her head back and forth as we ate. The waitress took my glass, took his bottle, and went to get us more drinks...

"So Harmony... are you coming from work?"

"Mmm hmmm..." I acknowledged as I continued eating...

"Where do you work?"

"I work in New York..."

"Where about?"

"Look at me – I'm making such a mess..." I said, deliberately avoiding her question...

"Here's some extra napkins..." the waitress said as she placed them on the table...

"Maybe you should slow down when you eat..." Helen said...

"Here's your drinks..." the waitress said as she placed them on the table...

"Here you go..." I said as I handed Harland his Guinness..."

"Thank you..."

"You're welcome..." Harland and I looked at each other, picked up our drinks, and took a sip...

"Harland – I'm ready to go..." Helen sighed...

"We're almost finished..." he said as we finished eating. Helen was sitting there fuming and I loved it...

"Will there be anything else?" the waitress asked as she came over...

"Not for me..." I answered...

"No thank you..." Helen answered...

"I'm good..." Harland answered...

"I bet you are..." I thought to myself as I finished my drink...

"What's wrong?" Harland asked...

"Nothing..." I sighed...

"Can we please go now?" Helen sighed...

"We can go as soon as she brings the check..." Harland answered...

"Helen – can you drive?" I asked...

"Why?"

"I was thinking about what you said – Harland shouldn't be driving..."

"He could drive just fine if he didn't have another drink!" she snapped...

"Harland – did they validate your parking?"

"He's parked on the street..." Helen answered...

"Why don't you drive the car – I know you're ready to go – I'll make sure Harland gets home..." I said...

"If I wanted to drive I would've driven..."

"I'm sorry – I was just thinking you were right – Harland shouldn't be driving..."

"He shouldn't've been drinking!" she snapped...

"This is Happy Hour..." Harland said...

"Gimmie the damn keys!" Helen snapped...

"Here you go..." Harland laughed as he placed the keys on the table... "I'll see you later

Mom...” he laughed as she got up and stormed out...

“Here’s your check...” the waitress said as she put the check on the table...

“Thank you...” Harland said as he put his card in the slot...

“I’ll be right back...” the waitress said...

“I have a confession to make...” I said...

“I’m listening...”

“I suggested your mother take the car on purpose...”

“I know...” he said as he smiled at me...

“You’re not mad?”

“I’m not – but she is...” he laughed...

“Sorry...” I said as I shrugged my shoulders...

“No you’re not...” he laughed...

“Here ya go – have a good night...” the waitress said as she put the check back on the table...

“Why was she here?” I asked...

“I didn’t invite her – she invited herself...”

“So... you couldn’t tell me?”

“Would you have come?”

“No...”

“That’s why I didn’t tell you...”

“Why didn’t you tell her it was our first date?”

“Is that what this was?”

“It would’ve been if your mother wasn’t here...”

"I'm sorry..."

"You owe me..."

"I'll make it up to you... if you let me..."

"I'll call you..." I said as his cell phone rang...

"Hello Mother... Yes I'm still here... I'll be leaving soon... No I'm not still drinking... Okay..."

"Did your mother make it home okay?"

"Yes..."

"Good – now I can make sure you get home... I said as I got up..."

"Wait..."

"Okay..." I said as I sat back down...

"Where do you work?"

"I work in New York..."

"Where in New York?"

"I work for Westchester County..."

"What do you do for Westchester County?"

"I prepare hearing calendars..."

"You work for the court?"

"No – I work in the office of fair hearings..."

"Fair hearings? As in DSS?"

"Yea..."

"You like it?"

"I do – but it's a lot of work – and my days are long – and when the bus is late or the trains are delayed – it's even longer..."

"You ever thought about transferring here?"

"You can't transfer from one state to another – if I did that, I'd lose my seniority..."

"Ooohhh – how many years do you have in?"

"Twenty seven..."

"Are you thinking about retiring soon?"

"I think about retiring every day..." I laughed...

"I work for the court house across the street..."

"Really?"

"Yea – that's why when you said you prepared hearing calendars, I thought you worked for the court house..."

"Did you grow up here?"

"Yea..."

"What do you do in the court house?"

"I work in the jury department..."

"Oh shit – please don't call me for jury duty!" I laughed...

"I don't have any control over that – but if anyone says they can't come due to extenuating circumstances, I process those..."

"You must be busy..."

"Very. Sometimes I don't get a break..."

"You don't get a break?"

"I get a lunch hour – but I don't always get to take it – especially when we're in the middle of jury selection..."

"So you work through lunch a lot?"

"Yea – they pay me for it though..."

"Well that's good at least..."

"Sure is..."

"How many years have you been there?"

"Twenty seven – same as you..."

"Are you thinking about retiring?"

"I do think about retiring – but I'm not ready to retire yet..."

"Why?"

"When I retire, I want to settle down..."

"Settle down? As in get married?"

"Yea..."

"Hmmm..." I said as I got up...

"Where are you going?"

"Home..." I answered as I took his hand, he got up from the table, and I led him outside...

"Let go of my hand..." I laughed...

"No..."

"I need my hand to get us an uber..."

"Okay..." he said as he let go of my hand. He watched me intently as I ordered the uber and put the phone back in my pocket... "You didn't ask me for my address..."

"I don't need your address..." I said as I took his hand. Harland didn't say anything. He just smiled and squeezed my hand... "This is us..." I said as the uber pulled up. Harland opened the door for me so I could get in. After he made sure I was good, he closed the door and went to get in on the other side...

"Harmony?" the driver asked...

"Yes Sir..." I answered. The driver drove off as Harland took my hand and squeezed it. We rode holding hands without speaking. When we got to my house, his cell phone rang again... "Give me your phone..." I commanded. Harland gave me his phone. I looked at it, saw his mother was calling, turned it off, and handed it back to him. Harland put the phone back in his pocket and we got out the uber...

"Good night Harmony..." the driver said...

"Good night..." I replied as the driver pulled off. I took Harland by the hand and we went inside...

"This is nice..." he said as he looked around...

"Take off your coat - make yourself comfortable..." Harland took off his coat, went over to the sofa, sat down, and put his coat beside him. I took off my coat, put it in my recliner, and went to stand in front of him...

"Come here..." he commanded as he pulled me towards him. I straddled his lap and climbed up on it. I could feel his dick against me as I lifted my skirt. He took my face in his hands, pulled me into a kiss, and pushed his tongue in my mouth. I welcomed his tongue as I opened my mouth further. He moved his hands behind my back and held me against him as we continued kissing for a few moments and then he moved his hands down to my ass and squeezed it...

"Huh..." I moaned in his mouth as he continued feeding me his tongue. I got wet as soon as I heard him unbuckle his belt and unzip his pants with one hand while palming my ass with the other. I wrapped my arms around him as I leaned into him, making it easier for him to move his hands up to my waist and rip my panties off. He rubbed his dick against my clit and just when I was about to cum, he grabbed my ass and thrust himself up inside me... "Huh... Huh... Huh..." I moaned in his mouth as he continued thrusting...

"Huh... Huh... Huh..." he moaned back in my mouth as we continued kissing sloppily...

"Huh... Huh... Huh..."

"Huh... Huh... Huh..."

"Shit... I'm cummin..."

"Cum for me..." he growled in my ear..."

HUH! HUH! HUH! HUH! HUH!"

"That's it... Gimmie that pussy! UGGH! UGGH! UGGH! UGGH! UGGH! UUUGGGHHH!!!"

"Come on..." I said as I got up off his lap and took his hand...

"Where we goin'?"

"Upstairs..." I breathed as I hurried upstairs and he hurried behind me...

"You don't wanna answer your phone huh – okay – I got something for that ass!" Helen snapped as she turned on the computer...

"Hurry up..." I breathed as I stretched out on the bed...

“I’m cummin’...” he breathed as he stripped down naked and climbed on top of me...

“432 Lindley Street – thanks GPS!” Helen exclaimed as she got in the car...

“Yes... Fuck me... Don’t stop...” I moaned...
“You want this dick?” Harland growled...
“Yes Harland – Yes!”
“Whose pussy is this?”
“Yours Harland – yours!”
“Damn right it’s mine!” he growled as he pulled out and flipped me over... “Get on your knees!” he commanded. I got on my knees, put my ass up, and put my head down on the pillow as Harland began pounding me from behind...
“Harland! Yes! Oh God! Fuck Me!”
“Uggh! Uggh! Uggh! Uggh! Uggh!” Harland’s balls were thumping against my clit as he continued slamming into me...
“Harland I’m cumming!”
“Cum all over my dick!”
“Aahh! Aahh! Aahh! Aahh! Aahh!”
“Uggh! Uggh! Uggh! Uggh! UUUGGGHHH!!!”

“You may not answer your phone – but I bet you’ll answer the fuckin’ door!” Helen gritted as she got out the car...

"Damn that was good..." Harland breathed...

"Hell yea..." I breathed as I fell down on the bed. Harland turned me on my back, laid down on top of me, and began kissing me...

"BANG! BANG! BANG!"

"Who the fuck is that?" Harland asked...

"I don't give a fuck..." I breathed as I pulled him back into a kiss...

"BANG! BANG! BANG!"

"I need to see who's banging on your door like that..." he said as he went to get up and I pulled him back down...

"What you need to do is give me some more dick..." I said as I pulled him into a kiss and spread my legs. Harland didn't pay the banging on the door any mind as he pushed his tongue in my mouth and began grinding himself into me. It wasn't long before his dick was hard and he was thrusting inside of me again... "Hmmh... Hmmh... Hmmh..."

"Hmmph... Hmmph... Hmmph..."

"Hmmh... Hmmh... Hmmh..."

"Hmmph... Hmmph... Hmmph..."

"HMMH! HMMH! HMMH! HMMH! HMMH!"

"HMMPH! HMMPH! HMMPH! HMMPH! HMMPH!"

"Damn..." I breathed...

"Was it good?"

"You tell me..."

"It was good..." he breathed as he started kissing me again...

"You wanna take a shower before you go?"

"Are you kicking me out?"

"I wouldn't say that..."

"What would you call it?" he laughed...

"I'm sorry – I need to get to bed – I gotta be up at 5..."

"What time do you report to work?"

"Eight..."

"What time do you get off?'

"Four..."

"No wonder you're tired..."

"Yea..."

"Do you really want me to leave?" he breathed as he started kissing me again...

"No..."

"So why am I leaving?"

"Because... I... won't... get... any... sleep..."

"You're right..." he said as he jumped up off me...

"You can use the towels in the bathroom – I'll get in after you get out..." I said as I sat up...

"Why don't you join me?"

"If I join you – you won't leave..." I laughed...

"You're right..." he said as he went into the bathroom and turned on the shower. I lay back on the bed and smiled as he started singing. I spread my legs, closed my eyes, and moved my hands down to my clit as he continued singing. I zoned out and began swirling my fingers around my clit. I was so into what I was doing I hadn't realized the he came out the shower and was standing there watching me. He tip toed over to the bed and pushed himself between my legs before I had a chance to react...

"Oh Harland..." I moaned as he devoured my clit. He moved his mouth and his tongue to the rhythm of my hips and didn't let up. I grabbed his head and ground my pussy into his face as my orgasm was building and when my legs started trembling, he sucked my clit hard... "Aaah! Aaah! Aaah! Aaah! Aaah!" I was sensitive and I tried to push Harland away from me but he wasn't having it...

"Mmm... Mmm... Mmm..." he moaned as he continued licking, sucking, and slurping. He continued devouring me as I rode out my orgasms on his face and then he stuck his tongue inside my pussy...

"Harland... Harland... Harland..."

"Damn your pussy tastes good..." he breathed as he went back to licking and slurping. I was in a state of euphoria. I didn't give a damn about anything... "Go get in the shower..."

"Huh?"

"Go get in the shower..."

"Okay..." I sighed as I sat up. Harland helped me up and I went to take a shower. When I got out the shower, he was completely dressed...

"I know..." he said as he pulled me into a kiss...

"Let me get my robe..." I sighed. I didn't want him to let go of me but he did so I got my robe and put it on. Harland took my hand we went downstairs...

"BANG! BANG! BANG!"

"I'm going to put a stop to this right now!" he exclaimed as he opened the door...

"Why the fuck didn't you answer your phone?" Helen snapped as she pushed her way in...

"Excuse me – I didn't say you could come in!" I snapped...

"Why the fuck didn't you answer your phone?" she snapped again, ignoring me...

"GET OUT!" I screamed...

"Answer me Harland!"

"GET THE FUCK OUT!" I screamed as I charged over towards her and just as I was about to push her out the house, he stopped me...

"Let's go..." he sighed as he guided his mother out the door. He turned to look at me, mouthed I'm sorry, and closed the door behind him...

Harland drove the car. His mother sat beside him smirking. As far as she was concerned, she won the battle. Unfortunately for her, she'd forgotten how powerful pussy was – especially mine. It had been a while since I had sex and that was by choice, because instead of having random sex just to keep from being horny, hot, and bothered, I was waiting for what I wanted. The Isley Brothers said it all in their song...

"Choosey Lover... Girl I'm so proud of ya... I'm so glad you chose me... and I'll make you so happy..."

Unbeknownst to Helen, her son knew this from the moment he touched me. When he grabbed me and kissed me, he knew I pushed him away because I liked it. It had nothing to do with him being arrogant – in fact, it was just the opposite. Unbeknownst to her, she lost the battle before the war got started. Unfortunately for us, she wasn't going to go away without a fight...

When they got in the house, Harland slammed the keys down on the table in the foyer...

"Don't you be slamming shit in my house!" Helen snapped. Harland turned around and looked at his mother with fire in his eyes. She was taken aback and afraid, but she wouldn't admit it...

"I will slam whatever the fuck I want to slam in my house!"

"Your house? Please..." she said as she tried to walk past him and flung her hand...

"Let me explain something to you..." he said as he grabbed his mother's hand and spun her around to face him... "I'll say it again – THIS IS MY HOUSE! I gave it to you but the title hasn't changed – and after what you pulled tonight – it never will..."

"Oh – I get it – you finally got some pussy so now you think you're the shit and you can just toss me aside..."

"I'm glad you understand..." he said as he let go of her hand and went towards the living room...

"Let me tell you one mutha-fuckin' thing..." she exclaimed as she followed him into the living room... "I don't care how knee-deep you are in the pussy – I am your mother – and..."

"And what?" Harland interrupted as he spun around so fast it surprised her... "I'll never toss you aside? Your problem is you're bitter – you take your issues with my father out on me – I'm sorry Dad hurt you but for God's sake – will you please go ride a dick 'cause after what you pulled tonight I'm convinced you're crazy!" Helen was stunned. She never thought her son would address her like that. She became enraged... she drew back her hand... and slapped him in his mouth so hard she drew blood...

"Don't you EVER talk to me like that again!"

"Truth hurts..." he said as he wiped his mouth...

"I don't give a fuck how good Harmony's pussy is – you will not disrespect me!"

"You know what – You're right – you don't have to put up with disrespect from me – you're my mother – in fact – maybe you should look for your own place – perhaps in a senior complex – this way you won't ever have to worry about me disrespecting you – I'm a grown man – I'm too old to be living with my mother – I should've been living on my own a long time ago – we'll talk about this more tomorrow – good night!" Helen stood there in shock. Harland got up, kissed her on the cheek, went upstairs to his room, and closed the door...

"Hey Harmony!" Snow exclaimed as she came into my Facebook room...

"Hey..."

"Wait a minute – why you look like you've been crying?!"

"Wait 'till Yyanna gets in here..."

"Fuck that – we gotta come through?!"

"Hey Harmony!" Yyanna exclaimed...

"Yyanna we might have to come through..." Snow said...

"What happened?!"

"Let's do a shot first..." I sighed...

"Oh shit – don't you have to work tomorrow?" Yyanna asked...

"I'm not going..." I said as I poured myself a shot of Captain Morgan...

"Hurry up and pour the damn shot – I'm tryin' to find out what the fuck happened dammit!" Snow laughed...

"Alright, alright – I'm pouring it – see?" Yyanna laughed as she poured her shot...

"Okay – drink!" I said as I gulped my shot down. I waited for Snow and Yyanna to drink their shots and then I spoke... "I called him..."

"Bout damn time!" Snow laughed...

"What man? What I miss?" Yyanna asked...

"She met him last week – they exchanged numbers – go 'head Harmony – I'm tryin' to find out what the fuck happened!" Snow laughed...

"He met me at the train station..."

"Okay..." they both said in unison...

"When I saw him I hugged him..."

"I thought you were gonna be careful and take it slow!" Snow exclaimed...

"That was me taking it slow..." I laughed...

"Okay – get to the good part!" Yyanna laughed...

"We went to Happy Hour at the Holiday Inn – and his mother was there!"

"His mother?" they both asked...

"Helen... from Hell..." I answered as I shook my head...

"Da fuck?" Snow asked...

"I would've left him right there with his mother!" Yyanna laughed...

"I was pissed – but it was his mother and I wouldn't want anyone to disrespect my mother so..."

"I understand that Harmony – but I'm with Yyanna – I would 'a left him right there with his mother!" Snow exclaimed...

"So he introduced me, we sat down, we order drinks. The waitress asks what we want and I told her just bring us everything on the appetizer menu..."

"Okay..." they both said...

"This Bitch gonna say don't you think you should've let her ask us what we wanted?"

"See – Harmony you good – I would 'a got up and left..." Snow said, shaking her head...

"I wanted to make nice for Harland..." I sighed...

"Damn Harmony – you feelin' him like that already?" Yyanna asked...

"Yea..."

"What happened after that – 'cause I already don't like her ass!" Snow exclaimed...

"I apologized..."

"Da fuck you apologizing for – see – I can't!" Snow exclaimed...

"Snow – let her finish!" Yyanna laughed...

"I'm sorry Harmony – go 'head..."

"I said I'm sorry – I didn't realize you'd be here and I told Harland I really wanted the appetizers..."

"So you got the appetizers..." Yyanna said...

"Not before she snapped at her son talkin' about you know those sliders come with bacon and you know I don't eat pork!"

"See – you good – I'm tellin' you – I would 'a left!" Snow exclaimed...

"What did he say?" Yyanna asked...

"I told the waitress she can bring us sliders without bacon..."

"So he didn't check him mother?!" Yyanna asked...

"Apparently not!" Snow exclaimed...

"So the waitress went to place our order and his mother asked how was your day... I said long... she says she was talking to Harland..."

"Harmony – why the fuck did you put up with that – fuck him – fuck her – no – just no!" Snow exclaimed...

"You must really be feelin' him..." Yyanna sighed...

"I thought I was showing him I could be respectful to his mother..." I said as I started crying...

"Harmony... No... Damn – I didn't mean to make you cry – I'm sorry..." Snow said as she started crying...

"Uh uh – stop that – I like it better when you're mad..." I said as I wiped my eyes...

"Okay – I'ma stop – go 'head..." Snow said as she wiped her eyes...

"So the waitress brought our drinks and I picked up my glass to toast to Happy Hour –

Harland picked up his bottle to toast with me – and his mother says I really think you should wait until you eat…"

"Well damn – is he fuckin' her?!" Snow snapped…

"Snow – you stupid!" Yyanna laughed…

"I'm just sayin'!" Snow snapped…

"So we toasted anyway and his mother was pissed!" I laughed…

"I don't understand why he didn't check his mother!" Yyanna exclaimed…

"That's what I'm saying!" Snow exclaimed…

"So the appetizers came and I start making my plate – and she says Harland aren't you eating?"

"So you were supposed to wait until he got his food?" Snow asked as she shook her head…

"I told him I gotchu and I gave him my plate…"

"Naa – you shouldn't have done that – he should've told you go 'head…" Yyanna said…

"Exactly!" Snow agreed…

"So I start making my plate and she says excuse me so I said we're splitting everything so I'll leave you some – and she says you could've waited until I was finished…" Snow was fuming. She punched her kitchen table and shook her head. Yyanna didn't comment so I continued… "The waitress came and I said I wanted another drink, Harland got another beer, and she says Harland – you're driving!"

"Did he say anything?" Yyanna asked...

"He told his mother I'll be fine... and girl..."

"What happened?" Yyanna asked...

"I was ready to fuck!" I laughed...

"I know that's right – 'bout damn time!" Snow laughed...

"How long as it been Harmony?" Yyanna asked...

"I stop counting after 12 months..." I sighed...

"Okay – I'ma need you to tell me you had a good night so I don't have to come through and beat a Bitch ass!" Snow exclaimed...

"Okay – so I was ready to fuck – so I asked her if she could drive..."

"Why would you ask her that? You can't get no dick if he goes home with his mother!" Yyanna laughed...

"I know!" Snow exclaimed...

"She asked me why so I told her I was thinking maybe she was right – he shouldn't drive..."

"Okay Harmony... I see you..." Yyanna laughed...

"She says if I wanted to drive, I would've driven!"

"See – I'm getting' mad again..." Snow said...

"Well she was mad 'cause she was ready to go and she wanted Harland to get up and take her home – but I wanted some dick so..."

"What happened?" Yyanna asked...

"She said gimmie the damn keys, Harland said here you go, and put the keys on the table!" I laughed...

"Okay – I'm startin' to calm down a little bit..." Snow said...

"So when she stormed out I asked him why she was there and he told me he didn't invite her but when she found out where he was going she insisted because she wanted to meet me..."

"Ooohhh... I get it..." Yyanna said...

"I don't!" Snow snapped...

"He told his mother about Harmony – she had to see who was pushing her out the top spot..."

"Oh shit!" Snow exclaimed...

"I went through that with my mother-in-law – we good now but in the beginning we bumped heads all the time..."

"How did you get good with your mother-in-law?" I asked...

"I cursed her out!" Yyanna laughed...

"See? That's what I'm talkin' about!" Snow exclaimed...

"Oh wait – I almost forgot – she asked me where I work and I told her I work in New York – she asked me where about – I changed the subject – I was expecting Harland and I would have a first date and we would get to know each other..."

"Did you tell him that?" Snow asked...

"I told him it would've been our first date if his mother wasn't there..."

"Exactly!" Snow exclaimed...

"So we talked for a while and got to know each other a bit and then I got up from the table and told him c'mon – we're goin' home..."

"Oh shit – you wasn't playin'!" Yyanna laughed...

"I ordered an uber and he said I didn't give you my address – I told him I don't need your address...

"Oh shit – Harmony said you gon' give me some dick!" Snow exclaimed...

"Basically..." I laughed...

"Okay – I'm feelin' better now..." Snow said...

"It won't last long..." I said...

"What happened now?" Yyanna asked...

"His mother called before we left and he's on the phone talkin' 'bout yes I'm still here, no I'm not still drinkin' – and she called him again after we got in the uber..."

"Dick-Blockin-Bitch!" Snow exclaimed...

"I told him give me your phone – I saw it was her calling, I turned the phone off, gave it back to him – and he put it in his pocket..."

"Hot damn!" Snow exclaimed...

"I thought you were gonna tell us he called his mother back..." Yyanna laughed...

"I told him to make himself comfortable so he took off his coat and sat down on the sofa – and then I made myself comfortable – and I sat on his dick..."

"Yeesss! That's what I'm talkin' about!" Snow exclaimed...

"Girl! Was it good?" Yyanna asked...

"Oh my God!" I exclaimed... "It was so good I took him upstairs!"

"Aww shit!" they both exclaimed...

"And then we heard somebody bangin' on the door..."

"Wait, wait, wait, wait, wait!" Snow exclaimed... "I know you not fixin' to tell me..."

"He said somebody's at the door – I told him I didn't give a fuck..." I interrupted...

"Okay!" they both exclaimed...

"We get back to it – we hear bangin' again – he says I need to go see who's at your door – I told him what you need to do is give me some more dick!"

"Aww shit!" they both exclaimed...

"We doin' our thing and when we finished I told him to go take a shower – he didn't wanna leave..."

"You fucked him and put him out?" Yyanna asked...

"Kinda..."

"Yo – that's fucked up!" Snow laughed...

"Snow – I told him I had to get up for work and if he stayed I wouldn't get any sleep..."

"Oh so you wanted him to stay..." Snow said...

"Yea..."

"I'm confused – you said you're not going to work – Snow said you look like you've been crying..." Yyanna said...

"After he got out the shower he got down between my legs and I fucked his face..."

"Aww shit!" they both exclaimed...

"I went to take a shower..."

"Did he come with you?" Yyanna asked...

"Naa – if he did – we'd still be in there..." I laughed...

"I'm so confused..." Snow said...

"After I got out the shower I put on my robe – he got dressed – we went downstairs – and BANG! BANG! BANG!"

"NO!" Snow exclaimed..."

"He said I'm going to put a stop to this right now – he snatched my door open – and it was his mother!"

"What the fuck – how the fuck – I can't!" Snow exclaimed...

"What'd he do?" Yyanna asked...

"This Bitch asks him why didn't you answer your fuckin' phone and pushed her way into my house!"

"Harmony – you better than me..." Snow started to say...

"I said – excuse me – I didn't say you could come in – she ignores me and says why the fuck didn't you answer your phone – I said get out!"

"I would've told her get the fuck out!" Yyanna snapped...

"She still ignoring me talkin' 'bout answer the fuckin' question Harland – so I screamed GET OUT! Now! and I charged towards her..."

"You put your hands on his mother?" Snow asked...

"I was going to – but he stopped me..."

"I would never put my hands on Flick's mother – but if she came in my house on that shit – I'on know..." Snow said...

"He guided his mother out – turned to me – mouthed I'm sorry – and closed the door behind him..."

"See – fuck him – fuck her – no – he should've checked his mother right there – she disrespected him – she disrespected you in your house – da fuck!" Snow exclaimed...

"I agree with Snow..." Yyanna said...

"I don't know what to do..." I sighed...

"You don't have to do a damn thing!" Snow snapped...

"I feel sorry for him – I know he feels bad – I wanna let him handle it..."

"He ain't handle shit!" Flick exclaimed...

"Oh shit – you heard that?" Snow asked as Flick came up behind her...

"Harmony – I wasn't eavesdropping – well – actually – I was – y'all talkin' about riddin' dick n shit – I couldn't help it – but if my mother ever came in my house and spoke to my wife like that – I'd put her ass out!"

"Thank you Baby..." Snow said...

"I understand you feel sorry for him – he was in a bad spot – I get that – but if he can't check his mother – maybe he's not the man for you..."

"Now I really don't know what to do..." I sighed...

"My wife already wants to come through – I can come through with her and have a talk with him if you want..."

"I love y'all..." I said as I started crying...

"Don't cry Harmony – he's not worth it..." Yyanna said...

"Yes he is..." I sighed...

"Harmony – listen – if you wanna give him another chance – that's up to you – but you need to check him and tell him to check his mother..." Flick said...

"Alright y'all – I'ma go – I need to try and get some sleep..."

"Okay good night..." Yyanna said...

"Good night Harmony!" Flick said as he left the kitchen...

"Good night..." Snow said as I left the room...

"I didn't get much sleep. I decided to get up and make myself some coffee. I turned over to look at the side of the bed where Harland was and even though I was sad, I began to smile. I slept with my phone next to me and kept it charged in case he sent me a message. Maybe I was dickmatized – but I didn't give a damn. It just couldn't end like this before it began. He has to make it up to me – we need to have a real date – a first date – without his mother...

"Bzzz! Bzzz! Bzzz!" I grabbed the phone and saw I had a text message from Harland...

"Harmony..." he started with a sad emoji face... "I'm sorry. I had no idea my mother was coming. I wanted to be with you so bad, it hurt. I was so happy when you took my phone from me and turned it off because that let me know you wanted to be with me too. You are something special and I don't want what happened last night to ruin what we shared before we get a chance to be happy. I'd like to come see you tonight to talk – if you're willing to hear me out. If you'd rather not see me again – fuck it – I can't lie – I need to see you... please..." he ended his text with another sad emoji and praying hands. I was on cloud nine. I held the phone close to my breast and imagine him sucking it...

"See – nope!" I said out loud as I went downstairs. I put the phone down, I went into the kitchen, and I made myself some coffee. After I sat down and started drinking my coffee, I replied to his text...

"Harland..." I started with a smiling emoji... "What happened last night was a lot to deal with. I was expecting to have a first date with you and I was also expecting we'd talk and get to know each other. I've wanted to be with you ever since the night you kissed me (I'm sure you knew that) – that's why I hugged you when I saw you. I didn't sleep well last night so I stayed home today. I'd love to see you so we can talk. What time do you get off work? Let me know and I'll meet you – I know you're at work but we can meet for lunch if that's okay…" I ended my text with a smiling emoji…

"You have made my day! What would you like for lunch?"

"Actually – I'd like some breakfast – I've been craving shrimp & grits and a steak, egg, & cheese sandwich from Queens Delight…"

"I'm on my way!"

"On your way? I thought you were at work?"

"I'm clocking out – I'll see you soon…"

"Okay…"

"What the fuck did I just do?" I sighed… "Oh well – good think I took a shower last night – I hope he doesn't wanna go out 'cause I'm not getting dressed…" I laughed as I finished my coffee. I turned on HGTV and whatever was on was watching me because I was barely paying attention. I was so happy I wanted to call Snow and Yyanna but I didn't because, to be honest, I was afraid they'd talk me out of it. I kicked back in my recliner and fell back to sleep…

I jumped as soon as I heard him knock... "Who is it?"

"Harland..." I jumped up out the recliner, hurried to the door, and snatched it open. Harland picked me up, I wrapped my legs around his waist, I wrapped my arms around his neck, and we tongued each other down as he walked inside and pushed the door closed with his foot. We continued kissing as he walked me over to the couch and sat me down. My legs were still wrapped around him as he got on his knees, opened my robe, took my breasts in his hands, and alternated between sucking the left nipple and the right...

"Harland..." I moaned. His tongue felt so good I arched my back so he would take more of my breast into his mouth. Harland was happy to oblige me and sucked on both of them so hard he left hickies on them before he started kissing his way down my stomach... "Huh... Huh..." I moaned. When he got to my pussy, he ran his tongue from the top of my clit down to the bottom and then he stuck his tongue inside... "Harland..." I moaned... and then he did something I've never had done before... and it startled me. Harland turned his head, took the left side of my labia into his mouth, and sucked it while sliding his tongue up and down... "Ooohhh..." I moaned...

"You like that?"

"Yeesss..." Harland turned his head to the right, took the right side of my labia in his mouth, and sucked it while sliding his tongue up and down... and then he took my clit in his mouth and sucked it... "Ooohhh... Yess... Harland..." I moaned. Harland stopped sucking, spread my lips, and flicked his tongue directly on my clit...

"OOOHHH... OOOHHH... OOOHHH... YEESS... FUCK!" Harland swirled his tongue around my clit and each time he swirled his tongue around, he applied more pressure... "HARLAND... DON'T STOP... DON'T STOP... I'M CUMMING!" I screamed as I grabbed his head and fucked his face. Harland continued swirling his tongue around my clit while applying pressure, giving me mini-gasms as I continued to ride his face. After I released my grip on his head, Harland stuck his tongue in my pussy and I laughed when he started slurping. Harland looked up at me and when he went to enter me, I stopped him...

"What's wrong?"

"Bring it to my mouth..." I breathed as I laid my head back and opened my mouth. Harland kicked his shoes off, stood up on the couch, lowered his dick to my mouth, and I took it in...

"Ohhh shiiittt!!!" he moaned as I swirled my tongue around the head and sucked simultaneously. Harland let me control the pace as I took more of his dick in my mouth... "Yes... Suck it... Yeessss..." I grabbed the bottom of his shaft and began sucking sloppily on his dick while simultaneously swirling my tongue on it... "Harmony... Shit... Suck it..." I let go of his dick, palmed his ass with my hands, and pushed him all the way in... "FFUUUCCCKKK!" he moaned. He began fucking my mouth slowly at first, allowing me to get used to the length and girth. When I pushed him in deeper, he knew what I wanted... "Take this dick!" he growled as he began fucking my mouth harder. I relaxed my throat and did as he commanded. I felt the vein on the side of his dick rising and I knew he was close to cumming... "Fuck... Shit... I'm cummin'... I'm cummin'... Uuuggghhh!" I held him in my mouth as he convulsed, swallowed his cum, and kept on sucking... "Harmony..." I looked up at him as he played in my hair and I continued sucking him softly. I began sucking a little more when I felt him getting hard again and he stopped me... "Let me fuck you... please..." he breathed. I looked up at him and eased my mouth off his dick until I got to the head. I wrapped my hand around his dick and held it as I flicked my tongue on the head of it... and Harland lost it... "I said I wanna fuck you!" he growled as he snatched his dick away from my mouth, held my legs up, and thrust himself inside me...

"Harland... Harland... Harland..." I moaned...

"Uugh... Uugh... Uugh..."

"Fuck me Harland... Just like that... Yesss..."

"Uugh... Uugh... Uugh..."

"Harder... Yes... Fuck... I'm cumming..."

"Uugh... Uugh... Uugh..."

"HARLAND!" I screamed as I came...

"UUUGH! UUUGH! UUUGH! UUUGH! UUUGH!" Harland stayed inside me and pushed his tongue in my mouth...

"Hmmph... Hmmph... Hmmph..." I moaned as he fucked out his orgasm. We began sucking each other's tongues and after a few moments I spoke... "Harland..."

"Yes Baby..."

"Where's the food?"

"Oh shit – I left it in the car!" he laughed as he got up. When he stood up, I inched over to the edge of the couch and took his dick in my mouth before he could *zip* his pants... "Now see – you startin' trouble again..." he breathed as he grabbed my head and pushed his dick in my mouth. I braced myself on the edge of the couch and let him fuck my mouth as much as he wanted to... and then he stopped suddenly...

"Why'd you stop?"

"I need to get the food..." he said as he turned away from me and went to get the food. I laughed when I saw him zip his pants before he went out the door. When he came back inside with the food, he locked the door and went into the dining room. I got up and followed him... "I hope it's still hot..." he said as he took the food out the bags and put it on the table...

"It is..." I said as I picked up the tins and felt underneath them...

"Good – 'cause I promised you breakfast..." he said as he went to sit down and I put my hand out to stop him... "I can't sit down?"

"Nope... I answered as I pulled him towards me and unzipped his pants. Harland looked down at me and smiled as I took his dick out and looked up at him... "Now... where were we?" I asked as I put his dick in my mouth. Harland didn't need to be told what to do – he grabbed my head and fucked my mouth...

"Mmm... Mmm... Mmm..." I moaned on his dick as I slurped...

"Fuck! Suck my dick!" I relaxed my jaws and took him all the way in as my spit ran down his balls... "I'm cummin'... I'm cummin'... I'm cummin'... Ffffuuucckkk!" Harland held my head as I swallowed and continued sucking softly until I pulled my mouth away... "Come here..." he commanded as he pulled me up from the chair and kissed me hard...

"Let's talk..." I breathed...

"Okay..." We sat down, opened the tins, opened the aluminum foil, and started eating. We didn't talk at all until we finished everything...

"Damn that was slamming – thank you!"

"Thank you..."

"For?"

"For wanting me..." he breathed as he leaned in and kissed me again...

"Let's talk..."

"Okay..." he sighed... "My mother is manic-depressive. When she takes her medication – she's okay – when she doesn't – she behaves like she did last night..."

"Harland – I'm sorry – I had no idea..."

"I know you didn't – but that's no excuse – my mother knew exactly what she was doing..."

"How do you deal with that?"

"As long as it's just me and her – she's fine – but now that you've come into my life – she feels threatened – when she feels threatened – she lashes out..."

"So she wants you all to herself?"

"Pretty much..."

"Well she needs to move over – 'cause I want you..."

"Harmony..." he whispered as he teared up...

"Don't cry..." I said as I leaned over to hug him...

"I'm so happy right now – it's been so long..."

"It's been a long time for me too..."

"I told my mother she needs to get her own place..."

"Harland no – don't put your mother out because of me..."

"I love you for saying that – but I didn't put her out because of you – well you were part of the reason – I put her out for me..."

"Are you sure?"

"Last night was the straw that broke the camel's back – she needs to go..."

"I'm sorry..."

"You don't need to apologize – I should've put my mother in her place a long time ago – plus – I'm a man – I don't need to be living with my mother anyway..."

"Why are you living with your mother?"

"I wasn't – at first – I have a 2-bedroom downtown – but my father left my mother because she's too controlling..."

"He didn't know she was manic-depressive?"

"He didn't give a damn – my mother plays on that – she can be very manipulative and controlling..."

"I'm so sorry..."

"When he left, he turned the house over to me but I gave it to her..."

"You're so sweet..."

"I gave it to her – but everything's still in my name – I pay the bills in both places..."

"You are really good to your mother..."

"I love my mother – I know you wanted to hurt her last night – and you had every right – but I couldn't let you..."

“Harland – all I was going to do was push her out of the house...”

“And she would’ve swung on you – and you would’ve been fighting...”

“Oh hell yea – you right...”

“I’ll still take care of my mother – but after last night – she has to go...”

“I wish it didn’t have to come to that...”

“Don’t feel bad – I don’t...”

“You don’t? Why?”

“She slapped me so hard she made my mouth bleed...”

“Oh my God! Why?”

“Because I told her she needed to go ride a dick...”

“Harland!”

“Well she does!” Harland laughed...

“How did she know where I lived?”

“I had a GPS tracker put in our phone after my father left – I need to be able to get to her if there’s an emergency...”

“Oh so when you didn’t answer your phone, she turned on the GPS tracker...”

“Yea...”

“So what happens now?”

“You take me upstairs...” he answered as he got up and then he pulled me up into his arms... “You let me make love to you...” he breathed as he kissed me... “You let me fuck you...” he breathed as he kissed me again... “We get in the shower...” he breathed as he kissed me again... "We fuck in the shower..." he breathed a she kissed me again... "We get out the shower..." he breathed as he kissed me again... "We go back to bed..." he breathed as he kissed me again... "And we do it again..." he breathed as he kissed me again... "And again..." he breathed as he kissed me again... "And again..."

"Okay!" I squealed as I took him by the hand and pulled him out the dining room...

"Harland – we need to talk..." Helen said as he came in...

"You wanna talk – let's talk..." he said as he took his coat off and sat down on the couch...

"I'm sorry for the way I acted..."

"Apology accepted..."

"Do you forgive me?"

"Of course I forgive you – but you're still moving out..."

"Harland..." she said as she sat next to him and took his hand in hers... "Please... don't make me leave... I promise – I won't do it again – I'll even apologize to Harmony..."

"I'm glad you want to apologize to Harmony – you owe her that – but you're still moving out..."

"Harland – I'm your mother – I don't have anywhere else to go – please don't do this..."

"Ma – listen to me..."

"Okay... I'm listening..."

"I am your son – I'm not your man..."

"I never said..."

"Let me finish..."

"Okay..."

"I love you – I've been taking care of you – I will continue to take care of you – but you're moving out..."

"This is because of Harmony – I wish you never met her ass!"

"See? This is what I'm talking about – you don't ever want to take responsibility for your behavior..."

"If you never met Harmony – none of this would be happening..."

"You still don't get it – this was going to happen one day – you had your time with Dad – I stepped up and I've been taking care of you – and I will still take care of you – but it's time for me to take care of me..."

"Why can't you be with Harmony and I stay here? Why do I have to move out?"

"I'ma tell you like you told me when I graduated from college – it's time for you to get the hell on up outta here so I can play house – in my house!"

"So this is about privacy?"

"You know what – I'm done – I'ma start looking at some studios and 1 bedrooms – I'll see if I can find something downtown so we can be close to one another and I can still check up on you..."

"Check up on me?"

"Ma – I said you were moving out – I never said I didn't want to see you again..."

"So I can come visit?"

"Of course!"

"You said you were going to put me in a senior complex..."

"Ma – I'm just looking out for you – I want you in a building with an elevator, handicap access – in a way this will work out well for you because you won't have to walk up and down the stairs..."

"I guess..." she sighed...

"Ma – how many times have you said you wish you could walk around bare-assed?"

"I've said that a few times..."

"Well – now you can walk around bare-assed all you want..." he said as he got up, went over to the computer, turned it on, and went to realtor.com...

"Mutha fucka think he puttin' me outta my got damned house – he got another thing coming!" Helen cursed under her breath as she made herself a plate of food in the kitchen... "I don't give a damn – I'll die before I let him move that Bitch in here..."

"Oh wow..." Harland exclaimed as he opened the listing... "$94k – price dropped by $5k – let's see why..." he said as he clicked on the picture... "Built in 1929... listed for 100 days... walking distance of shops, restaurants, metro north... oh shit... this is my building! Perfect! I love it! I'll see if I can do a Hubbard Clause – if they're willing to do that, I won't have to pay mortgage and maintenance on two places – now let's see what my monthly payment is going to be... oh shit – this is only going to cost me $500 a month – yeeesss!"

"Ma?"

"Yes Harland?"

"I wanna invite Harmony over for dinner..."

"You wanna invite Harmony here?"

"Yes..."

"Umm... why?"

"I wanna give you a chance to apologize – and I want us all to have a do-over..."

"You wanna have her over for dinner – that's fine..." she said as she rolled her eyes..."

"Okay – is tomorrow alright?"

"Doesn't matter what day you do it – you're cooking..."

"Okay – tomorrow it is..."

"Now I gotta make nice with this Bitch!" Helen mumbled under her breath...

"Hey..." I answered...

"Hey..." he breathed...

"I miss you..."

"Is that right?"

"Yea..." I breathed as I ran my hands across my breasts...

"What are you doing?"

"It's what you're doing..." I breathed as I moved my hand down to my pussy...

"What am I doing?"

"You're rubbing your dick on my clit..." I moaned...

"Is it good Baby?"

"Yeesss..."

"What am I doing down?"

"Fucking me..." I moaned as I put two fingers in my pussy and began fucking myself...

"How's my dick feel?" he breathed as I laid back in the recliner and spread my legs...

"Oh God... Harland... your dick feels so good..." I moaned as I pushed my fingers in deeper...

"Put my dick in your mouth and taste yourself..."

"Mmmm..." I moaned in the phone as I sucked my fingers...

"Suck my dick..." he breathed. I sucked my fingers sloppily so he could hear me slurping...

"Now put my dick back in your pussy so I can fuck you hard..."

"Ohhh... Harland... Fuck... I'm about to cum..."

"Not yet..."

"Not yet?"

"Slow down..."

"Okay..."

"I wanna fuck you slow... long... deep strokes..." he breathed as he got up, went upstairs, went into his room, and closed the door...

"Where are you?" I breathed...

"I'm in my room... I have my dick in my hand... and I'm imagining my dick inside you..." he breathed as he stroked himself...

"Oh Harland... I wanna cum..."

"Not yet Baby... I'm imagining my dick going in deeper... Shit... You're so fucking wet..."

"Harland... Please let me cum..."

"Take my dick out your pussy and put it in your mouth for me – I wanna hear you suck it..."

"Mmm... Mmm... Mmm..."

"That's it... Suck it... Fuck..."

"Harland... Make Me Cum... Please..."

"Put my dick back in your pussy Baby..."

"Oh Harland... Huh... Huh... Huh... I'm cumming..."

"I'm cumming inside your pussy Baby..."

"Huh... Huh... Huh... Huh... Huh..."

"Uggh... Uggh... Uggh... Uggh... Uuuggghhh!"

"Mmm... Mmm... Mmm..."

"Is it good Baby?"

"Yeesss... It's good..."

"Tomorrow I'll give you the real thing..."

"You will?"

"I will... but I need you to do something for me..."

"I'll do whatever you want..."

"I want you to come over for dinner..."

"You want me to come to your house? For dinner?"

"Yes..."

"Will your mother be there?"

"Yes..."

"Umm... are you sure about this?"

"Yes..."

"I want to... but I'm scared..."

"My mother wants to apologize to you..."

"Uh huh..."

"So you'll come?"

"If you give me some dick I will..."

"I want you to pack an overnight bag..."

"It's one thing to come for dinner – now you talkin' about me spending the night... in the house... with your mother..."

"Do you trust me?"

"It's not you I'm worried about..."

"I'll make it worth your while..."

"Okay..."

"You'll come?"
"I'll come... all over that dick of yours..."
"Now see... you startin' trouble again..."
"Harland?"
"Yea Ma?"
"Are you in your room?"
"Yea!"
"Whatcha doin'?"
"I'm on the phone..."
"Le'me let you go..." I laughed...
"You still coming tomorrow – right?"
"All over that dick..."
"Bye!" he laughed...

"Hey yall!" I exclaimed as they came into my room...

"Aww shit – she's smiling – she got some more dick..." Snow said...

"Yea... I did..." I sighed...

"So you gave him another chance?" Yyanna asked...

"Yea..."

"Harmony – I know you're happy – I'm happy for you – I just want you to stay happy..." Snow said...

"What happened Harmony?" Yyanna asked...

"I stayed home from work yesterday..."

"Okay..." they both said...

"He text me..."

"What'd he say?" Snow asked...

"Le'me read it to y'all..." I answered and then I began reading...

"Harmony... I'm sorry. I had no idea my mother was coming. I wanted to be with you so bad, it hurt. I was so happy when you took my phone from me and turned it off because that let me know you wanted to be with me too. You are something special and I don't want what happened last night to ruin what we shared before we get a chance to be happy. I'd like to come see you tonight to talk – if you're willing to hear me out. If you'd rather not see me again – fuck it – I can't lie – I need to see you... please..."

"Damn!! You got him beggin' n shit!" Snow exclaimed...

"Yea..."

"I ain't gonna front – I would 'a gave him the pussy too..." Yyanna said...

"I ain't gonna front – me n Flick get into it – he apologizes – I apologize – we fuckin'!" Snow laughed...

"Le'me read all the texts to y'all..." I said and then I started reading again...

"Harland... what happened last night was a lot to deal with. I was expecting to have a first date with you and I was also expecting we'd talk and get to know each other. I've wanted to be with you ever since the night you kissed me (I'm sure you knew that) – that's why I hugged you when I saw you. I didn't sleep well last night so I stayed home today. I'd love to see you so we can talk. What time do you get off work? Let me know and I'll meet you – I know you're at work but we can meet for lunch if that's okay..."

"You have made my day! What would you like for lunch?"

"Actually – I'd like some breakfast – I've been craving shrimp & grits and a steak, egg, & cheese sandwich from Queens Delight..."

"I'm on my way!"

"On your way? I thought you were at work?"

"I'm clocking out – I'll see you soon..."

"Okay..."

"Fuck it – I'm done – I would 'a gave him my body and told him do whatever you want!" Yyanna laughed...

"I did!" I laughed...

"I'm still not sure about him Harmony – men can talk the talk when they fucked up..."

"Speaking of that – boy did we talk..."

"Oh shit..." Yyanna said...

"Did you curse him out?" Snow asked...

"No... I hugged him..."

"You hugged him? Why?" Snow asked...

"His mother is manic-depressive..."

"Oh shit!" they both exclaimed...

"Yea..."

"Damn – now I wanna give him a hug – got me wantin' to come through and beat his mother's ass – I still wanna beat her ass though..." Snow said...

"I wanna give him a hug too – that's hard on anybody..." Yyanna said...

"He said when she takes her medication she's good – but when she doesn't take her medication – she acts out..."

"So what – he has to take care of his mother forever?" Snow asked...

"He doesn't have to – but he wants to..."

"I can understand that..." Yyanna said...

"He's putting his mother out..."

"Oh shit – what?" Snow asked...

"Oh yea – I told him don't put her out because of me but he said I was only part of the reason..."

"Damn..." Yyanna said...

"She was still goin' off when they got home – they got into it – he told her she needs to go ride a dick – she slapped him in his mouth so hard she drew blood..." They both bust out laughing...

"I'm sorry..." Snow laughed... "I don't mean to laugh... but... wait... I can't!"

"Harmony – what if he's just telling you that to string you along?"

"I'll find out tomorrow..."

"Why? What's happening tomorrow?" Snow asked...

"He invited me over for dinner..."

"Is his mother gonna be there?" Yyanna asked...

"Yes..."

"Uh uh Harmony – I dunno about that..."

"He said his mother wants to apologize..."

"Really?" they both asked...

"That's what he said..." I sighed...

"Harmony – I'm tellin' you right now..." Snow started to say...

"I know, I know – if some shit jump off – get the fuck out – fuck him – fuck her!"

"I hope everything goes okay tomorrow..." Yyanna said...

"Me too..." I sighed...

"She can apologize if she want to – I still don't trust her ass!" Snow exclaimed...

"I don't either..."

"You don't?" Yyanna asked...

"Hell no!"

"Okay Harmony – I see you..."

"She already showed me who she really is – I'll accept her apology for Harland – but I'll never trust her..."

"I know that's right!" Snow exclaimed...

"Alright y'all – it's past my bedtime – good night..."

"Good night!" they both said as we left the room...

"Hey!" Harland exclaimed...

"Hey..."

"Where are you?"

"I'm pulling into Bridgeport now..."

"Good – I need to take you somewhere before we go to the house..."

"Okay – I'm on my way down..." I said as I got in the elevator...

"Hey!" Harland exclaimed when he saw me. I didn't get a chance to hug him because as soon as he saw me, he picked me up in his arms and spun me around...

"Where are you taking me?"

"You'll see..." he said as he pulled me across the street to his car. After he opened the door and I got in, he closed the door and we were on our way. I got curious when I saw we were on Lafayette Street... "We're here..." he said as he parked the car. I waited for him to open the door before I got out... "Come with me..." he said as he took my hand and we went inside the building...

"Good evening Mr. Wilkins..." the doorman greeted...

"Good evening Charles – could you let me in unit 2J?"

"I'm not supposed to let anybody in there – but I'll make an exception for you..." he said as he got in the elevator with us...

"Why does he need to be let into his own place?" I thought to myself...

"We're here..." Harland said as he took me by the hand and led me to the door. Charles opened it for us and I saw Harland slip him $100... "Thank you Charles..." he said as he closed the door... "C'mere..." he breathed as he pulled me into a kiss and pushed his tongue in my mouth. He picked me up, put me on the counter, dropped down on his knees, and pushed my legs apart...

"Harland... Huh..." I moaned as he began devouring me. He licked, sucked, and slurped for a while and just as I was getting ready to cum... he stopped... "Why'd you stop?" I panted. He didn't answer me – he picked me up off the counter, put me down on the floor, took me by the hand, and pulled me into the bathroom... "Turn around..." he commanded. I did as I was told as I stood in front of the mirror... “Hold on to the sink...” he commanded. I did as I was told... “Spread your legs...” he commanded. I spread my legs and braced myself as he lifted my skirt, positioned himself behind me so I could see him fuck me from behind, and slammed his dick inside me...

“Harland! Oh shit! Fuck me!”

“What did you tell me last night?” he growled as he pounded...

“I... wanna... cum... all... over... your... dick!”

“Cum for me...”

“Huh... Huh... Huh... Huh... Huh... Harland... I’m cumming... I’m cumming... HHHUUUGGG!!!”

“Uggh! Uggh! Uggh! Uggh! UUUGGGHHH!!!”

“Thank you...” I panted... I needed that...”

“You’re welcome...”

“Harland?”

“Yes Harmony?”

“Umm... why are we here?” I asked as I turned on the water, soaped the washcloth, and began washing up...

“I’m buying this condo for my mother...”

“Oh wow – does she know?”

“No – I’m not telling her yet...”

“Oh shit – did I just use her washcloth?” I laughed...

"No – I just put that out – don't worry about it though..." he laughed... "I'll put out a fresh one..."

"What are we going to do with this one?" I asked as I held it up. He didn't answer me – he took it out of my hand, wiped his face with it, put it over his nose, inhaled deeply, and then he put it in his pocket...

"You're not wearing any panties..."

"I know..."

"C'mon – I'll show you the bedroom..." he said as he took me by the hand and led me to the bedroom...

"This is nice – and big..."

"Yes it is..."

"Do you think your mother will like it?"

"I know she will..."

"I hope so..."

"C'mon..." he said as he took me by the hand and pulled me towards the door...

"Okay..." I laughed as we left the condo and got in the elevator. When we got downstairs, we went outside and he took me on the side of the building... "Where are we going now?" I asked. Harland didn't answer me. I watched as he opened the door and went inside...

"You comin'?" he asked as he turned around to look back at me...

"I'm coming..." I answered as I hurried up the steps and into the condo...

"This is my condo..."

"I tried..." I sighed as he started the car...

"I know... I'm sorry..."

"Do me a favor?"

"Sure..."

"Stop apologizing for your mother..."

"Okay – I'm sorry you didn't enjoy yourself..."

"I really enjoyed your food..."

"Thank you..."

"I didn't get anything to drink..."

"I'll give you something to drink when we get to my place..." he said as we turned onto Lafayette Street...

"We're here..." I said...

"Yes we are..." he acknowledged as he parked the car. I didn't wait for him to come open the door for me – I got out, grabbed my overnight bag, closed the door, and looked down the street... "What are you doing?"

"I'm just wondering how long it's going to take me to walk to the train station..."

"You're not walking to the train station..."

"Okay..." I sighed as he took my hand and we started walking towards the private entrance...

"What time is your train?"

"I can get the 6:38 or the 6:50..." I answered as he opened the door and I went inside...

"What train would you like to get?" he asked as he came inside behind me and closed the door...

"I'd like to get the 6:38 train..." I answered as I went towards the bedroom...

"Okay..." he said as I got undressed... "I'll set the alarm for 5... and we'll leave at 6..." He watched me as I folded my clothes, put them in the bag, pulled out a night gown, and put it on... "Are you going to bed already?"

"Oh no – when I'm ready for bed I don't wear anything..."

"So you sleep naked?"

"Yea..."

"You sure you don't wanna go to bed now?" he asked as he came up behind me and grabbed my breasts in his hands...

"Not yet... I'm thirsty..." I breathed as I laid my head back on his chest and enjoyed his massage...

"I'll get us something to drink... and then I want us to go to bed..."

"Okay..." I sighed as I followed him into the kitchen...

"What would you like to drink?"

"Do you have Pepsi?"

"You don't want anything else?"

"Naa – I don't drink during the week..."

"Okay – Pepsi over ice coming up..." he said as I sat at the table. He took two glasses out the cabinet, filled them with ice, poured Pepsi in them, put the cap back on the bottle, picked up the glasses, and sat at the table with them...

"Thank you..." I said as I picked up the glass and started drinking..."

"So you don't drink during the week?" he asked as he took a sip...

"Once in a while – but most of the time – no..."

"Why not?"

"It makes it harder for me to get up in the morning..."

"Can you cook?"

"I can cook a little..."

"Maybe one day you'll cook a lil' somethin' for me..."

"I might... but right now I'm going to enjoy your cooking..."

"You said a man that can cook turns you on..." he said as he got up from the table...

"Yes..."

"Are you turned on right now?" he asked as he came closer to me...

"Yes..."

"Are you ready to go to bed?" he asked as he took my hand...

"Yes..." I answered as I got up from the table. Harland started to walk me towards the bedroom and I pulled away from him...

"What's wrong?"

"I'm just locking the door..." I said as I slid the bolt into the lock. Harland came over to me, took my hand, and led me to the bedroom. As soon as we got in the bedroom, I took off my nightgown and got in the bed...

"Are you comfortable?"

"Very..." I answered as I watched him get undressed... "Do you sleep naked?"

"No..."

"Why not?"

"I like pajamas..."

"You're not going to put on pajamas right now – are you?"

"Is that a problem?"

"Naa – I'll just ask you to take them off..."

"I won't put any on..." he laughed as he came over to the bed and got in. I moved over towards him and snuggled up underneath him... "Do you mind if I smoke?"

"You smoke?"

"Yea..." he said as he opened the nightstand and pulled out a blunt...

"I don't mind..." I sighed...

"It helps me relax after a long day..." he said as he lit it and took a pull from it...

"Don't they do random drug tests at your job?"

"I never have to worry about that..."

"I do..."

"You don't have anybody you can ask to pee in a cup for you?"

"They talk too much at my job – besides – I haven't smoked weed since high school...

"Sit up..." I sat up and looked at him...

"Smoke this with me...

"Ask me on Friday..."

"C'mon – just take one pull..."

"Put it in your mouth..." Harland did as he was told... "Shotgun..." Harland blew a shot into my mouth and then he took it out of his mouth and handed it to me... "Finish it..."

"I'm good – you finish it..." I coughed. Harland finished the blunt and then he pulled me into a kiss. He was kissing me so sensually I started to wonder who I was in bed with until he stopped kissing me and reminded me...

"Get on your back..." I got on my back with the quickness and spread my legs. Harland got on top of me, lay down, and whispered in my ear... "What was it you imagined me doing to you?"

"I imagined you rubbing your dick against my clit..."

"Like this?" he asked as he began rubbing his dick against my clit...

"Yeesss..." I panted...

"What else was I doing to you?"

"You were fucking me..." I breathed as he put his dick inside me and began thrusting...

'What did I tell you to do next?"

"You... told... me... to... Huh..."

"Answer me..."

"You... told... me... to... take... your... dick... and... Oh God..."

"And what?"

"Huh... taste... myself!" I moaned. Harland took his dick out my pussy, brought it to my mouth, and moaned when I took it in my mouth...

"Yeesss... Suck it..."

"Please make me cum..." I panted. Harland moved down, got on top of me, and began fucking me again... "Harland... Yes... Fuck me..."

"Uugh! Uugh! Uugh!"

"Fuck me! Don't stop! I'm cumming! I'm cumming!"

"Uuugh! Uuugh! Uuugh! Uuugh! Uuuggghhh!!" Harland collapsed on top of me and fell asleep...

"It's 5 a.m...." Siri said as Harland's cell phone began the waking music. Harland was sleeping so hard he didn't hear it. I got up, turned the alarm off, and went to get in the shower. I turned the shower on, got in, and looked at the door a few times to see if he was going to join me... "Oh well..." I mumbled as I turned off the water, got out, and dried off. I looked at the door as I brushed my teeth to see if he was going to join me but he didn't... "Oh well..." I mumbled again as I went back into the room, put on deodorant, and got dressed... "Hmm – it's 5:30 – I hope he has coffee..." I said as I went into the kitchen... "Oh thank God – Maxwell House..." I breathed as I turned on the kettle. The kettle whistled, I made myself a cup of coffee, sat down at the table, and drank my coffee as I watched the sun come up... "I'm sure it's 6 now..." I said as I got up to go look at my cell phone... "Have a good day..." I whispered as I picked up my cell phone, my charger, my purse, and my coat and then I left. I got to the train station at 6:30. I got on the elevator, got off at the platform, and bought my ticket on the app. As soon as I was done buying my ticket, my phone rang... "Good morning..."

"Why didn't you wake me?"

"You didn't hear the alarm..."

"I'm sorry – I'm not used to getting up at 5 a.m...." he yawned...

"That's my train coming Babe – I'll call you later..."

"Okay – have a good day – I love you..."

"I love you too..."

"Hey guys!" I exclaimed as they came into the room...

"You're smiling – is that good?" Yyanna asked...

"Yes..."

"Are you sure Harmony?" You don't look as happy as you did the other night..." Snow said...

"Well – Harland said he wanted to take me somewhere before we went to his mother's house for dinner..."

"Okay..." they both said...

"Well – he takes me to see a condo..."

"Oh so you went to his house?" Yyanna asked...

"No – the doorman had to let us in – Harland slipped him $100..."

"Oh shit – what the hell?" Snow asked...

"What the hell is right!" I laughed...

"Y'all was fuckin'?"

"Oh yea..."

"I'm confused – he took you to a vacant condo – to fuck?" Yyanna asked...

"He took me to the condo he's buying for his mother..."

"Oh shit – y'all fuck in his mother's house!" Snow laughed...

"Girl – I was washing my ass when he told me – I asked him if it was his mother's wash cloth!" I laughed...

"Oh my God – was it?' Yyanna asked...

"No – it was brand new..."

"You didn't leave it in there – did you?" Snow asked...

"No..."

"Thank God!" Snow exclaimed...

"Does she know he's buying that for her?" Yyanna asked...

"No..."

"You gonna tell her?"

"I'm staying outta that..." I answered...

"How was dinner?" Snow asked...

"Le'me tell you what happened when we went downstairs..."

"Downstairs?" Yyanna asked...

"He has a two-bedroom on the ground floor..."

"He's buying his mother a condo in the building he lives in?" Snow asked...

"Yea..."

"Oh hell no – I hope he's not thinking you'll move in with him..." Yyanna said...

"He hinted at it..."

"Are you serious?" Snow asked...

"The other day when we talked – he said when he retired he wanted to settle down..."

"Settle down? As in get married?" Snow asked...

"Yea..."

"Oh shit!" they both exclaimed...

"He suggested that the 2nd bedroom could be my office..."

"Harmony – please listen to me..."

"Snow – I'm not moving in with him – especially with his mother on the 2nd floor..." I interrupted...

"Oh hell no – I wouldn't move in either!" Yyanna exclaimed...

"I'll spend the night – but I'm not moving in..."

"Why does he want his mother on top of him like that though?" Snow asked...

"I looked up the property..."

"Aww shit – see – that's what I'm talkin' about!" Snow exclaimed...

"I think he's buying in his building because it's affordable..."

"Damn – he can swing two mortgages?" Yyanna asked...

"He won't have to – he's going to sell the house his mother's in – he'll probably pay off both mortgages with the money – at least that's what I'd do..."

"Is the maintenance high?" Snow asked...

"He can cover his mother's expenses for $500 a month..."

"Oh shit – that's cheap?" Snow exclaimed...

"I thought he lived with his mother?" Yyanna asked...

"He does..."

"So he's already paying two mortgages..."

"Yea..."

"Damn – Harmony hit the jackpot – good dick and money!" Yyanna exclaimed...

"I know that's right!" Snow laughed...

"So about dinner..." I sighed...

"Here we go!" Snow exclaimed...

"We go inside – I say hello Helen – she says hello but doesn't even bother to look up at me..."

"See – I'm getting' mad – he's not checkin' his mother..." Snow said...

"Exactly!" Yyanna agreed...

"I said thank you for inviting me to dinner – she says I wasn't the one that invited you..."

"What the fuck – did he check his mother?" Snow asked...

"He checked her..."

"Bout damn time!"

"Right!" Yyanna agreed...

"He says let's go eat – we go into the dining room – he asks his mother if she coming – she says I already ate – y'all took too long..."

"I swear to God I wanna beat her ass!" Snow exclaimed...

"I don't like to call anybody's mother out their name – but she's just an evil Bitch!" Yyanna exclaimed...

"I asked her to come sit with us..."

"Why?" Snow asked as she rolled her eyes..."

"For Harland..." I sighed...

"Did she come to the table?" Yyanna asked...

"Yea..."

"Well did you eat?" Snow asked...

"Did I – Harland brought me a plate of meatloaf, string beans, baked macaroni & cheese, and candied yams!"

"Okay!" they both exclaimed...

"So I said oh my God – this looks delicious! - this Bitch gonna say - did you really think we'd give you nasty food?"

"What?!" they both exclaimed...

"See – I can't – I'm tellin' you – I would 'a left them in that damn house!" Snow exclaimed...

"I said you never know how food is until you taste it – I started eating - I said oh my God - this is so good – Helen – you're a good cook – Harland says thank you..."

"Oh shit – he cooked all that?" Yyanna asked...

"He cooked all that – so I said I love a man that can cook – this Bitch gonna say is that because you can't cook?"

"I wanna beat her ass... I wanna beat her ass... I wanna beat her ass!" Snow exclaimed as she banged her fist on her table...

"Harmony – what did you say?" Yyanna asked...

"I said it's not because I can't cook - it's because a man that can cook turns me on..."

"I know that's the fuck right!" Snow exclaimed...

"Now she wants to apologize – so she apologizes..."

"Well that's nice..." Yyanna said...

"I said I accept your apology – she gonna say you don't have anything else to say?"

"I don't get it – what the fuck else were you supposed to say?" Snow asked...

"I said no – she gonna say don't you think you think you owe me an apology?"

"Why the fuck do you owe her an apology?" Yyanna asked...

"I know you didn't apologize to her..." Snow said...

"Absolutely not – I got up and took our plates and put them in the sink – I start to go back in the dining room – this Bitch gonna say umm – where do you think you're going – so I said I'm coming back in the dining room to sit with you and Harland – she goin' say you left dishes in the sink..."

"Oh hell – see – I can't... I can't... I can't!" Snow exclaimed...

"Did you wash the dishes?" Yyanna asked...

"Hell no! I asked her was I supposed to put them somewhere else – she goin' say we don't leave dishes in the sink in this house..."

"Harmony – I'm tellin' you..." Snow started to say...

"I told Harland I was ready to go – and then I left – this Bitch talkin' bout buh bye! and waived!"

"Yo – I'm sorry – that's so fucked up!" Yyanna said as she shook her head...

"So... wait – Flick – bring me my drink..." We waited for Flick to bring Snow her drink...

"Hey Harmony..." he said...

"Hey Flick..."

"You good?"

"I'm great!"

"Okay – just checkin'..." he said as he walked away and Snow took a sip of her drink...

"So... you mean to tell me... this mutha fucka let his mother talk to you like that... and then he let you leave... and he didn't check his mother... and he didn't come check on you either?"

"He stopped me before I walked out the door – he told me to wait – I said what am I waiting for – he said me – he handed me the keys to his car – I got in the car – and he came back out..."

"Oh okay – I'm feeling a little bit better – not much – just a little..." Snow said...

"I still think he could've checked his mother before it got to that point..." Yyanna said...

"I told him I tried – he said I know – I'm sorry – I said do me a favor – stop apologizing for your mother..."

"I know that's right!" Snow exclaimed...

"You gonna try again?" Yyanna asked...

"Hell no!"

"Good – I wouldn't try again either!" Snow exclaimed...

"When we got to his place, he gave me something to drink... and then he said so you said a man that can cook turns you on – so are you turned on right now?"

"Aww shit!" they both exclaimed...

"We went in the room – he lit a blunt – we smoked it – and let's just say I forgot how good sex is when you smoke..."

"Okay!" they both exclaimed...

"It was on – I didn't think about his mother and neither did he!" I laughed...

"So you spent the night..." Yyanna said...

"I spent the night – I got up the next morning, took a shower, got dressed, made some coffee, and walked to the train station..."

"He didn't take you to the train station?"

"He never woke up!" I laughed...

"Oh damn! That must 'a been some strong weed!" Snow exclaimed...

"It was – I only took a shotgun – he smoked the rest..."

"Shotgun?" Yyanna asked...

"That's when you blow a shot in someone's mouth and they suck it in..." I explained...

"Okay – I feel better now – you had a good night – but I have a question..."

"Yes Snow?"

"I know you said you wasn't moving in with him – but what if – after he sells the house and everything – he wants you to move in with him? What about when you spend the night – his mother's gonna be right upstairs – can you put up with that?"

"Snow – I have plenty of experience closing doors in people's faces..." I laughed...

"Okay!" Yyanna laughed...

"Harmony – that's all good – I hear you – but what if he doesn't let you close the door in his mother's face?"

"Then he can sleep with his mother – and I can go home..."

"You say that now..."

"Snow – after tonight – it will only take one time – if any shit like that happens – I'll tell him I'm not coming back to your house – I'm not putting up with that shit – after tonight – I'm done!"

"I hear you Harmony!" Yyanna said...

"Okay – I hope you mean that..." Snow said...

"If I forget – please remind me..." I laughed...

"Okay – remember what she said Yyanna!" Snow exclaimed...

"Oh God!" Yyanna laughed...

"Well ladies..."

"It's past your bedtime!" Yyanna laughed...

"Yea..."

"Good night Harmony..." Snow said...

"Good night Harmony..." Yyanna said...

"Good night – love y'all..." I said and then we all left the room...

"This is Sheddi Lemdon..."

"Hello Ms. Lemdon – my name is Harland Wilkins – I'm calling you because I'm interested in purchasing one property – selling another property – and doing a hubbard clause..."

"Okay – let's start with what you want to buy..."

"I live at 881 Lafayette Blvd, Unit 1B, in Bridgeport. I want to buy Unit 2J in the same building..."

"Do you want to sell your condo?"

"No – I want to sell my house at 1266 Laurel Avenue in Bridgeport..."

"Do you have a mortgage on the house?"

"No..."

"I see the condo you're interested in has been on the market for over 100 days – I'm not sure if they'll do a hubbard clause..."

"They might do it if they know I'm the buyer..."

"If they're not willing to do the hubbard clause, do you still want the property?"

"Absolutely – but I do have a request..."

"What can I do for you?"

"I don't want my mother to know I'm selling the house until after I get an offer..."

"Is she on the title?"

"No – but the house is her only connection she has left to my father..."

"I understand..."

"I believe she'll be happy when she finds out we'll be in the same building..."

"I'm sure she will be..."

"I'd like to list the house immediately..."

"Can I put a sign outside?"

"I'd rather you wait until we move out..."

"Okay – do I have your permission to show the property?"

"Yes – I'll give you access..."

"Okay – I'll let them know you'd like to make an offer – can we meet later today?"

"Sure – what time?"

"I get off at 5 – I work at the court house – how about we meet at the Holiday Inn in the lobby?"

"I'll see you at 5..."

"Mutha fucka thinks he's slick – runnin' outta here not washing these fuckin' dishes – you wanted to invite the Bitch over for dinner – you wanted to cook for her – you fuckin' clean!" she snapped as she threw a plate across the room and shattered it... "Shit – le'me clean this up before he gets home..."

"Ms. Lemdon?" Harland asked as he stood up...

"Mr. Wilkins – how'd you know it was me?"

"I recognized you from your photo..." he answered as they both sat down...

"Okay – I have some papers I need you to sign..." she said as she pulled out a folder...

"Okay..."

"This is an agreement between you and me – basically it says you agree that I'm your realtor – you can agree to 3 months or 6 months..."

"I'll sign it for 6 months..."

"That's fine – but I want you to read it first..." she said as she handed it to him. Harland read it, signed it, and dated it... "Okay – I'm going to sign it, date it, and give you a copy..."

"Okay..."

"Now – this is the contract for the condo – I specified you'd like to do a hubbard clause – but if they say no – are you prepared to come up with 20 percent?"

"I can do that..."

"Okay – I want you to read this first – then sign it and date it – I can't give you a copy yet – I'm going to present the offer – if they accept, then their realtor will fill in their information, they'll fax it back to me – you sign it – we fax it back..."

"Okay..."

"I'll also need a check for 1 percent to go with the offer..."

"That's fine..." Harland said as he read over the contract. He signed the contract, took out his check book, wrote her a check, and gave them both to her...

"Okay – now there's one more thing..."

"Okay..."

"As a realtor, I normally charge 6 percent – but that's negotiable..."

"Six percent of the property I'm selling?"

"Yes..."

"What about the property I'm buying?"

"Their realtor pays me for bringing them a buyer..."

"Okay..."

"Do you have an attorney?"

"I do..."

"Okay – text me their information – I'll need it..."

"I can do that..."

"If they don't accept the hubbard clause you'll need to get pre-approved - but this property isn't expensive and you own two other properties so I don't think that will be a problem..."

"I'm sure it won't..."

"Mr. Wilkins – it's been a pleasure..." she said as she extended her hand...

"Please call me Harland..."

"Harland – please call me Sheddi..."

"Thank you Sheddi..."

"You're welcome – I'll call you tomorrow..." she said as she left...

"Hey Harland..."

"Hey – where are you?"

"I'm about to get off the train..."

"Meet me at the Holiday Inn..."

"Oh God – is your mother there?"

"No..."

"You promise?"

"I promise..."

"I'll see you soon..." I sighed before I hung up...

When I got to the hotel, I looked to the left and right before I went into the lobby. Harland laughed at me as I walked over to him and sat down...

"You can laugh at me all you want..."

"My mother's not here..." he laughed...

"Not yet..."

"I didn't invite her..."

"You didn't invite her to my house either..." I sighed as I rolled my eyes...

"Can we start over?"

"Okay..."

"Hi..." he breathed as he pulled me into a kiss...

"Hi..." I breathed...

"I invited you here for a celebration..."

"A celebration?"

"Let's get a table..."

"Welcome to Park City Grill – table for 2?"

"Table for 3..." Helen said as she came up behind us...

"Hello Mother..." Harland said...

"Hello Helen..." I said...

"Hello..."

"Right this way..." the hostess said as we followed her to a table and sat down...

"Pomegranate Martini, Margarita, and Guinness – right?" the waitress asked as she came over...

"Right..." I answered...

"Same as before?"

"I'd like everything on the happy hour menu – my mother-in-law doesn't eat pork though – so we'll take the sliders with no bacon..."

"Did you say mother-in-law?" the waitress asked...

"Yea..."

"Congratulations..."

"Thank you..." I gushed...

"Harland! Do you have something you need to tell me?" Helen asked...

"As a matter-of-fact – I do..."

"When's the big day?" she sighed...

"I just listed the house today – we don't have an offer yet..."

"What?!"

"I put the house on the market today..."

"You did that without discussing it with me?"

"Mother – we had a discussion – don't you remember?"

"You told me I would be able to come by and visit!"

"And I meant that – you can come by and visit us at the condo..."

"Us?" Helen and I both asked in unison...

"You can stay with me temporarily until I find you a place – once you move out – Harmony's moving in..."

"This some bullshit – you know what – fuck this – I'm outta here!" she snapped as she got up and stormed out. I tried to hold it in but I couldn't help it...

"Aaaa Haaaa! Aaaa Haaaa! Aaaa Haaaa!" Harland tried not to laugh but it didn't work...

"Aaaa Haaaa! Aaaa Haaaa! Aaaa Haaaa!"

"Here's your drinks..." the waitress said as she placed them on the table... "Where'd your mother-in-law go?"

"She had to leave..."

"Oh shoot – I'll take this..." she said as she went to pick up the margarita..."

"Leave it!" I exclaimed...

"Okay..." she laughed...

"Thank you..." I breathed as I pulled Harland into a kiss...

"For what?"

"For checking your mother..."

"We need to talk about that..."

"Wait..." I said as I picked up the margarita and gulped it down...

"You know my mother will stop by – right?"

"Harland – if your mother stops by to visit you – that's fine – I don't expect you to cut your mother off completely – but I don't expect her to just pop in whenever – tonight is a perfect example – she tracts you using the GPS and just pops up – I don't want her doing that whenever she feels like it – and you shouldn't either..."

"You're right..."

"You told me she wasn't here – you told me she wasn't coming – and here she was!"

"You're right – but I'm glad she showed up..."

"Why?"

"After I went back in the house last night, she expected me to wash the dishes..." he laughed...

"Oh shit – are you serious?"

“I’m serious – I told her when you cook, I wash the dishes – tonight I cooked, you can wash the dishes...” he laughed again...

“Are you giving your mother a key to your condo?”

“My mother doesn’t have a key – and she won’t be getting one...”

“Okay...”

“Here’s your appetizers...” the waitress said as she placed them on the table...

“Thank you...” I said...

“Will there be anything else?”

“We’re good...” Harland answered...

“Harland – I’m not moving in...”

“I know...”

“Let’s see how it goes with your mother being right upstairs...”

“What if I want to invite my mother for dinner?”

“See – this is why I’m not moving in...”

“It’ll just be once in a while...”

“Can we stop talking about your mother – please!”

“Okay...” he said as he kissed me... “Are you coming over tonight?”

“Not tonight – I wanna go home...”

“Can I come?”

“Yea...”

“Can I stay? Please?”

“Yea...”

“Yea?”

"Yea..."

"Oh yea!" he exclaimed as he mimicked the wrestler Macho Man Randy Savage and I laughed...

"Mutha fucka think he can sell my house? Guess what – I'm not leaving – and you can't put me out – wait a minute..." She stopped talking out loud and started thinking... "He said I can move in with him temporarily – all I have to do is tell him I don't like whatever he shows me – that Bitch will never be able to move in! Aaaa Haaaa! Aaaa Haaaa! Aaaa Haaaa!"

"I need to get comfortable..." I said as soon as I got in the door... "Give me your coat..."

"Here..." he said after he took off his coat. I put our coats in the closet, came back out into the living room, and immediately started getting undressed... "Going to bed already?" he asked as he smiled at me mischievously...

"Naa – I do this every day..." I answered as I stripped down and put on my robe... "Here – take your clothes off and put this on..." I commanded as I handed him a robe... "Sorry I don't have any pajamas..."

"I can sleep naked tonight..." he laughed...

"If you get any sleep..."

"Are you telling me you might keep me up all night?" he asked as he came up behind me, untied my robe, and ran his hands down my waist as he began kissing me on my neck...

"Maybe..." I breathed as he moved his hands up to my breasts and began massaging them...

"Let's go upstairs..." he breathed in my ear...

"Okay..." I breathed. I took his hand and led him upstairs... "There's Pepsi, ginger ale, and water in the fridge if you're thirsty..."

"I didn't even notice that..."

"We were focused on other things..." I said as I led him to the chairs at the end of the bed and turned on the television...

"What are we watching?"

"Chicago Med..."

"I like Chicago Med..."

"I watch them all..."

"Me too..."

"Chicago P.D. is my favorite..."

"Mine too..."

"You wanna go to bed?"

"I'd love to – but if I go to bed right now, I'll get comfortable – and I'll fall asleep..."

"Are you really that tired?"

"I had two drinks and a plate full of appetizers..."

"I can keep you awake..."

"Yes you can – and Chicago Med will end up watching me..." I laughed...

"Is that because you won't be able to keep your hands off me?"

"Oh yes – that's it – I won't be able to keep my hands off you..." I laughed. Harland stood up, took off his robe, and stood in front of me with his hands on his hips...

"Fuck it..." I sighed as I stood up, took off my robe, went over to the bed, and got in. Harland got in bed behind me and when he pulled me close to him, I could feel his erection pushing against my ass... "Oohhh..."

"Uh uh – Chicago Med is on..." he said as he began massaging my breasts...

"Harland – stop it..."

"What?" he breathed in my ear as he ran his hands down my body and then he put his hand between my legs...

"Nothing..." I answered as I turned to face him, ran my hands down his body to his dick, and then I began massaging it...

"Like I said..." he breathed as he pushed me on my back, climbed on top of me, and thrust himself inside me... "You... can't... keep... your... hands... off... me..."

"Huh... you're... right... Huh... I... Can't..." I panted as I spread my legs wider, grabbed his ass, and pushed him in deeper...

"Yeesss..." he breathed as he lay down and pushed his tongue in my mouth. I wrapped my legs around his back and locked my ankles behind him as he began fucking me harder...

"Mmmh... Mmmh... Mmmh..."

"Mmmph... Mmmph... Mmmph..."

"Mmmh... Mmmh... Mmmh..."

"Mmmph... Mmmph... Mmmph... "

"MMMH... MMMH... MMMH... MMMH... MMMH..."

"MMMPH... MMMPH... MMMPH... MMMPH... MMMPH..." I kept my ankles locked behind his back as we continued kissing. After a while, I unlocked my ankles, relaxed my legs, reached for the towel I kept on the end table, and passed it to him. After he cleaned himself, I started getting horny again as he cleaned me too. He smiled as he noticed me getting wet again, but he didn't react as I expected – he put the towel behind us, pulled me to him, and we began watching Chicago Fire... "I love you..." he whispered in my ear...

"I love you too..." As we were watching television, I started thinking about moving in with him. I'd been by myself for so long I'd forgotten how good it felt to fall asleep in the arms of someone you love. I got comfortable in my thoughts and just as I started to relax, his phone rang... "Is that who I think it is?" I asked as I sat up...

"Only one way to find out..." he answered as he got up and went to check his phone... "Yea..." he answered... "I can do that... Okay... I'll see you at 8..." he said before he hung up...

"Who was that?" I asked...

"Work..."

"You have to go in early?"

"Yea..." he answered as he climbed back in bed and spooned me...

"What time?"

"8..."

"Do you need to get up before 5?"

"Naa – I can drop you at the train, go home, shower, change, and get there by 8..."

"You sure?"

"You're not trying to put me out are you?'

"Hell no..." I breathed as I turned to face him and pulled him into a kiss. The rest of the night was an orgasmic blur. I don't remember watching anything but when the television went off, I knew we had to stop... "I... need... to... get... some... sleep..."

"Okay..." he panted...

"Oh my God..." I groaned as Siri began singing...

"Good morning..." he breathed as he pulled me into a kiss...

"Good morning – I need to get up..." I said as I tried to pull away from him and he pulled me back towards him...

"You... need... to... stay... here..." he kissed...

"Harland – I can't..." I said as I jumped up, turned Siri off, and went to get in the shower. I was standing under the water when I saw him peeing and my eyes were glued to his dick. Harland caught me looking at him, turned to the side, and shook his dick while stroking it... "Uh uh – I gotta get to work..." I laughed as I turned away from him. When I got out the shower he was still standing there... "Harland – stop it – I need to get ready for work...

"What am I doing?" he asked as he came up behind me. I put on deodorant, put toothpaste on my toothbrush, and brushed my teeth. When I bent over to spit in the sink, Harland grabbed me and thrust himself inside me... "Harland... Fuck..."

"You know you want this dick!" he growled as he pounded me - and he was right – I wanted it... "Fuck me... Just like that... Yes!"

"Cum for me!"

"Huh... Huh... Huh... Fuck... I'm cumming... I'm cumming... Aaaaah!"

"Ugh! Ugh! Ugh! Ugh! Uuuggghhh!"

"Shit – what time is it?" I panted...

"I'll get you there on time..." he breathed as he turned me around to face him and kissed me...

"Harland – let me go get dressed..."

"Okay..." he said as he stepped away from me. I took my washcloth, soaped it up, went over my pussy again, and then I went to get dressed...

"Shit – it's 6 – I gotta go!"

"C'mon – I'll throw on my clothes real quick – if we leave by 6:15 I'll get you there at 6:30..."

We got to the train at 6:30 and when I went to get out the car Harland pulled me back in...

"Excuse me... Miss?"

"Oh – sorry..." I said as I turned back to kiss him. He pulled me closer and kissed me hard...

"Have a great day... I love you..."

"I love you too..."

"I'll call you later!" he yelled as I hurried into the elevator...

"Where the hell were you?" Helen asked as Harland went inside his condo...

"How did you get in here?"

"Charles let me in..."

"Get out!"

"You're throwing me out?"

"Ma – go home!"

"Home? I don't have a home – you're selling it – remember?"

"You know what – I don't have time for this..." he said as he took his mother by the arm, opened the door, put her out, closed the door, and put the bolt on... "I'll deal with her later..." he mumbled as he stripped out of his clothes and went to get in the shower...

"Mutha fucka thinks he can just put me out my house and I won't do shit – I got something for that ass..."

"This is Harland..."

"Good morning Harland, this is Sheddi..."

"Good morning..."

"I have news..."

"So soon?"

"Yes – I'm sorry to tell you they won't do a hubbard clause..."

"That's okay..."

"The quickest way to get a pre-approval is to do one on line..."

"On line?"

"Yes – you click on the property you want – you click on apply for financing, you fill in the information, and they'll send you an email to let you know if you're approved..."

"Don't you need a complete application?"

"We can get that later – as long as you receive an email saying you're approved, I can forward that with the offer..."

"I'll do that in a few minutes..."

"Good – I'm trying to convince them not to take any more offers – you're offering full asking and you're waiving the inspection so that's a plus..."

"Yea – I know the building – there won't be any issues..."

"Okay – get that over to me asap..."

"Okay Sheddi..."

"What the hell is going on?" Helen asked as she got up to go look out the window... "Oh hell no!" she exclaimed as she snatched the door open and ran up to the man on the property... "Who the hell are you?"

"Maam?"

"I said who the hell are you?"

"I'm Mark from Better Homes and Gardens – I'm putting a sign up – this house is for sale..."

"On whose authority?"

"Maam – the listing agent's number is right there – have a great day..." he said as he walked away and left her standing there...

"Hello – this is Sheddi Lemdon with Better Homes and Gardens Realty. Please leave your name and number – I promise – I'll get back to you..."

"Hello Ms. Lemdon – this is Helen Wilkins – I believe there's been some sort of miss-understanding – my home is not for sale – please call me at 203-642-4859. Thank you..."

"Hello Sheddi..." Harland greeted...

"Harland – we have a problem..."

"What's wrong?"

"One of my associates went to put a sign on your property and your mother berated him..."

"Oh my God – is he okay?"

"He's fine – I'm just bringing it to your attention because if someone wants to see the property – I don't want any problems...

"You won't have any other problems Sheddi – I'll move my mother out this weekend..."

"What if they don't accept your offer until Monday?"

"I have two bedrooms – my mother can stay with me until they accept my offer..."

"Okay – I won't schedule any showings until after this weekend..."

"Thank you Sheddi..."

"You're welcome – have you heard from anyone yet?"

"Yes – I got two pre-approvals..."

"Great – forward them to me and I'll see what I can do about your offer..."

"I'm forwarding them now..." he said before hanging up...

"Hello?" Helen answered...

"Ms. Wilkins – this is Ms. Lemdon returning your call..."

"Thank you for calling me back – you need to take that damn sign out from in front of my house – 'cause it's not for sale!"

"Ms. Wilkins – I spoke with your son – everything's going to be okay..."

"Really?'

"Absolutely..."

"Thank you so much Ms. Lemdon..."

"You're welcome..."
"Have a good day..."
"You too..."

"Hi Honey!" I exclaimed...

"I really needed to hear your voice..." he sighed...

"What's wrong?"

"I don't wanna talk about it – can I see you later?"

"Where?"

"Wherever you want..."

"Come by my house – I'll cook you a lil' something..."

"What time?"

"It doesn't matter – just come by..."

"Okay – I'll see you later tonight..."

"Harland?"

"Yes Harmony?"

"Please don't bring your mother..."

"Trust me – I'm not!" he laughed and then he hung up...

I was on cloud nine. My supervisor left early so I went to see the assistant supervisor...

"Lorraine – I don't know what's going on with me but I can barely keep my eyes open – I'm going home..."

"Okay – see you tomorrow..." she said as she continued painting her nails. I clocked out and went straight to Shoprite. I decided I was going to make baked ziti and garlic bread with cheese. I got everything I needed, got the pan, went to the self-checkout, and left...

"I can get the 3 o'clock bus to Stamford – I'll get to Bridgeport at 5 p.m. instead of 6 p.m. – this is perfect!" I exclaimed as I hurried to the bus stop...

"This is Harland..."

"Harland – they accepted your offer..."

"Yeesss!"

"We can close in two weeks – I forwarded a copy of everything to your attorney and your email – I also sent you a list of everything you'll need to bring with you to the closing..."

"Thank you Sheddi..."

"I spoke to your mother earlier..."

"Oh boy..."

"She was a bit snippy but she calmed right down after I told her I spoke with you and everything will be just fine..."

"You're amazing!"

"Well thank you – but she isn't the first cranky person I've had to deal with..." Sheddi laughed...

"Thank you..."

"I have an appointment to show your home on Saturday – can you take care of your mother?"

"What time?"

"1 p.m...."

"Sure – I'll take her to lunch..."

"Okay – I'll talk to you soon..." she said as she hung up...

As soon as I got in the house, I took off my coat, stripped down, put my robe on, put my hair up, and went into the kitchen. I took everything out the bags, washed my hand, got the pots, the frying pans, and went to work...

"I can't believe she's cooking for me!" Harland exclaimed as he hurried out the courthouse. He was at my house in 15 minutes...

"Who is it?"

"It's Harland..." I went to open the door and barely got it open before we were all over each other...

"Close the door..." I panted as my robe opened...

"Mmm..." he moaned in my mouth as he kissed me hard and squeezed my ass..."

"Long day?"

"Yea... – le'me take off my coat – I'll tell you about it..." he said as he took off his coat and put it on the sofa... "Smells good..."

"Thank you..."

"What are you making?"

"Baked ziti and garlic bread with cheese..."

"I love baked ziti..."

"I added sweet Italian sausage – I hope that's alright..."

"That's fine..." he said as he went to sit in the dining room...

"You want a beer?"

"You got Guinness?"

"I got Guinness..." I answered as I went into the refrigerator, took out two bottles, opened them, and sat down at the table with him...

"My mother was in my condo when I got home..." he sighed...

"How did she get in?"

"Charles let her in..."

"I'm sorry Babe..."

"I won't have to deal with this much longer..."

"Really?"

"Sheddi called – they accepted my offer on the condo upstairs..."

"That's great!"

"Yes it is – now I can go ahead and sell my house..."

"How does she feel about that?"

"She went off on the guy that put the sign up at the house today..."

"I'm sorry..."

"I'm moving her in with me until we close on the condo upstairs..."

"Really?"

"Yes – I'm moving her in this weekend..."

"I guess I won't be there then..."

"I was hoping I could come here..."

"Until you close on the other condo?"

"No – Friday night..."

"You can come here Friday night..."

"I'm taking my mother out to lunch on Saturday..."

"That's nice..."

"I don't have a choice – Sheddi's bringing someone to look at the house and I don't want my mother there..." he said as the timer went off and I got up... "Need any help?"

"I got it..." I said as I went into the kitchen. Harland watched me intently as I took the baked ziti out the oven along with the garlic bread with cheese. I turned off the oven, made two plates, got two forks, and brought them to the table...

"This looks so good..." he breathed...

"Thank you..."

"Mmmm!" he exclaimed as he tasted it. I smiled as we ate. He started to relax as he enjoyed his food and that made me happy... "Thank you Baby – I needed this – I needed you..."

"I needed you too..."

"Oh yea?" he asked as he got up from the table and came over towards me...

"Yea..." I answered, looking up at him. Harland took my hand and motioned for me to get up. I got up and he moved me to a corner against the wall. When he opened his pants and took his dick out, I began to smile. He came towards me and lifted me up. I wrapped my legs around him, I wrapped my arms around his neck, and he thrust himself inside me... "Ohh... Ooohhh... Ooohhh..."

"Uuugh... Uuugh... Uuugh..."

"Harland... Yes... Don't stop..."

"Your pussy's so fuckin' wet... Damn!"

"Huh... Huh... Huh... HUUUHHH!"

"Uuugh... Uuugh... Uuugh... Uuugh... UUUUGGGHHH!" Harland put my legs down and pinned me up against the wall for a few moments and we began kissing as his cum ran down my legs...

"I wish you could stay..."

"Really?"

"Yes..."

"I wish I could too – but I need to talk to my mother..."

"I know..."

"This will be over soon – and then we can take turns cooking for each other..."

"I like when you cook..."

"I like when you cook..."

"I might as well put the food away..." I sighed...

"It'll be over soon... I promise..."

"I know..."

"I'll call you later tonight..."

"Okay..."

"I love you..."

"I love you too..." he said as he left. Something came over me and as soon as he closed the door, I burst into tears...

"Harland – I'm glad you're here – I spoke with Ms. Lemdon – I knew you'd take care of everything..." Helen greeted as she hugged him...

"Ma – I'm moving you in with me – all the furniture is going into a pods – the house is officially for sale..."

"I thought Sheddi said everything will be fine..."

"It will be – the pods will be here in the morning – I have a couple of guys coming to help out – I also have a dumpster going in the driveway – whatever you don't want is going in the dumpster – you'll be staying with me until we close on your new place..."

"You found me a place already? Where?"

"It's a surprise..."

"I don't get to see it?"

"You'll see it soon – I don't want to spoil the surprise..."

"Okay..." she sighed. Helen went into the living room, sat down on the couch, and started crying...

"Ma... stop crying..." Harland said as he pulled his mother into a hug..."

"You're selling my house!" she cried...

"Ma... it's time to let go..."

"I'm not ready..."

"I'll be right there with you..."

"No you won't – you're going to put me away somewhere – I'm never going to see you again..."

"I'm not going to do that to you Ma..."

"You promise?"

"I promise..." he breathed as he kissed her eyes..."

"I'm staying with you?"

"Yes Ma..."

"You're not going to put me out in the street?"

"Never Ma... I swear..."

"Can I bring my bedroom set?"

"Yes Ma..."

"Can I bring my living room set?"

"Yes Ma..."

"Cn I bring my dining room set?"

"I'm not sure it will fit..."

"Can we try?"

"Sure Ma... we can try..."

"Okay..."

"I'm staying home from work tomorrow and Friday so I'll be here to make sure everything goes smoothly..."

"Okay... Can I bring my clothes?"

"Yes Ma..."

"Okay..."

"I'm going upstairs to lie down..."

"You want anything to eat?"

"I already ate..."

"What'd you eat?"

"I had baked ziti and garlic bread with cheese..."

"Harmony cooked for you?"

"Yea..."

"Was it good?"

"Yea..."

"Okay..."

"I'm going upstairs now Ma..."

"Okay son – I love you..."

"I love you too..." he said as he went upstairs, went to his room, closed the door, and called me...

"Hey Babe..."

"Hey..."

"Harland... what's wrong?"

"I'm okay..."

"No... You're not..."

"Am I doing the right thing?"

"Absolutely..."

"You're not just saying that because you want me all to yourself are you?"

"Of course I am!" I laughed...

"I'm taking Thursday and Friday to get our things moved into the pods, the dumpster, etc..."

"You need any help?"

"You'd do that?"

"If you want me to..."

"That's sweet of you – but I think I should do this with my mother..."

"Can I see you on Sunday?"

"I don't know..."

"Oh wow... your mother didn't take it too well... did she?"

"She cried..." he answered as he started crying..."

"Harland... don't cry..."

"I can't help it..."

"Harland – do you remember what you told me?"

"I told you a lot..."

"You told me your mother knows what she's doing..."

"I dunno... this was different..."

"You also told me your mother can be very manipulative..."

"I don't think she was doing that Harmony...

"Just be careful..."

"I will... I'll talk to you later..."

"Harland... I love you...

"I love you too..."

"Works every time..." Helen said as she crept back towards her room...

"Harland!"

"Huh?"

"Somebody's at the door!"

"Oh shit – what time is it?"

"It's 8 o'clock..."

"They're here – go answer the door – I'll be down in a minute..." he said as he got up out the bed...

"Oh my damn – why are you naked – don't nobody wanna see that!"

"Oh please – you used to change my diapers..." he laughed as he got dressed...

"That was then – this is now!" she laughed...

"You wouldn't have to worry about any of that if you'd stop watching me and go answer the door..."

"Alright – I'm going!" she laughed as she went downstairs...

"Good morning!" she greeted...

"Ms. Wilkins?"

"Yes..."

"Where would you like the pods?"

"Harland?"

"I'm on my way down..." he answered as he came downstairs...

"Good morning – I'll show you..." he said as he went outside and the guys followed him... 'I want the pods on the right side of the driveway – the dumpster is going on the left side..."

"Okay Mr. Wilkins – just sign here and we'll do the rest – it'll take a few minutes..."

"Okay - thanks..."

"Harland – what do you need me to do?" Helen asked...

"Nothing at the moment – once they get the dumpster and the pods in the driveway, we can take our time – no rush..."

"No rush? I thought you said we had to be out by Friday?"

"We do Ma – it won't take long..."

"Harland – do you realize how much stuff is in here?"

"Ma – go sit down – I got it..."

"Fine with me..." she said as she went to sit in the living room...

"Mr. Wilkins?"

"Yea..."

"We're finished..."

"I'll be right there..." Harland said as he went outside...

"Sign here – this says you acknowledge receipt of the pods and the dumpster. Here's the key to the pods. You call us and let us know when you're ready for us to come pick them up...

"That's it?"

"That's it..."

"Okay – thanks..." Harland said as he took the receipt, signed it, put the lock and key in his pocket, took a copy of the receipt for himself, and gave them the original...

"Have a good day Mr. Wilkins..."

"Thank you..." Harland went back inside and smelled coffee... "Smells good..." he said as he sat down at the table. Helen brought two cups of coffee to the table and sat down...

"Thanks..."

"Harland..."

"Yes Ma?"

"Nothing... never mind..."

"I'm gonna miss it too..."

"So it's not just me?"

"It's not just you..."

"So why are you selling it then?"

"Because it's time..."

"I always thought you'd meet someone, fall in love, get married, and I'd be living here with my grandchildren..."

"Well... some of that happened..."

"What are you saying?"

"I wanna marry her..."

"You wanna marry Harmony?"

"Yea Ma – I wanna marry Harmony..."

"I want you to be happy..."

"You sure about that?"

"Of course – I always wanted you to be happy – I just want to be included in your happiness..."

"Ma – where am I sitting right now?"

"That's exactly my point – we won't be living together anymore – I want us to always be able to sit down and have a cup of coffee..."

"Ma – you can always have coffee with me – but you have to understand Harmony is a part of my life – and she isn't going anywhere..."

"Trust me – you're selling my house because of her – I know exactly who she is..."

"See? This is what I'm talking about – no matter what I do for you – no matter how much I take care of you – you don't think about anybody but yourself!"

"Harland – that's not true..."

"Yes it is! When we were young I used to watch you and Dad together and I'd always say I'm gonna find someone to love me and I'm gonna be just like my parents..."

"Really? I never knew that..."

"Well now you know... and now I have... and instead of being happy for me..."

"Harland..." she interrupted... "I get it – I'm sorry..."

"After what happened the other night – I'm not too sure..."

"I'll apologize to Harmony..."

"You already apologized to her – and it turned out to be a disaster..."

"Harland – I won't do it again – I promise – I tell you what – after we get settled you can invite harmony over for dinner again – and I'll behave – I promise..."

"Harland – you in there?"

"Shit – that's the door..." he said as he got up and hurried to the door... "Good morning – thanks for coming guys..."

"You're welcome – let's do this!" James said...

"Okay – we'll start with the garage – all that shit is going in the dumpster..."

"Harland – I need to go through..." she started to say...

"Ma stop – that shit has been sitting in the garage for years – if it was important – it would 'a been in the house..."

"So we cleaning out the garage?" Alex asked...

"Yea – everything in the dumpster..." Harland answered as they went to clean out the garage. It didn't take them long to clean out the garage and when they were done, Harland stepped outside and looked at it... "Damn – this garage hasn't been cleaned in a long time..." he sighed...

"You ready to go inside?" James asked...

"Yea..." Harland sighed...

"Guys – anybody hungry? I made breakfast..." Helen said...

"Thanks – but I wanna finish while I'm motivated..." Alex said...

"And I want you to have the energy to finish – come eat..."

"Yes Maam..." Alex laughed as he came to the table and sat down...

"Ms. Wilkins – this wasn't necessary – but I'm grateful – thank you..." James said as he sat down...

"You're welcome – it's the least I could do – I appreciate y'all..." she said as she put a plate of scrambled eggs, sausage, grits, and biscuits in front of them...

"Ma – you've outdone yourself..." Harland said as he sat down and she gave him a plate...

"Orange juice is in the fridge – y'all can help yourselves..." Helen said as she sat down and started eating with them. When they were finished eating, James got up and put his dishes in the sink...

"Umm – excuse me – we don't leave dishes in the sink in this house..." Helen said...

"Ma – I'll wash the dishes – we need to get back to business - let's head upstairs – Ma – did you clean out your drawers?"

"My drawers? What my panties got to do with this?" Everyone bust out laughing...

"Aaaa Haaaa! Aaaa Haaaa! Aaaa Haaaa!"

"Ma – the dresser drawers – not your panties!" Harland laughed...

"You didn't tell me I had to do all that!" Helen snapped...

"Ma – its fine – we'll take the drawers out the dresser – we'll put the dresser in the pods – then we'll put the drawers back in the dresser – c'mon guys!" he said as they followed him upstairs...

"Y'all be careful – you break a mirror – that's 7 years bad luck..." Helen said...

"Ma – we got it..." Harland said as they took the dresser downstairs...

"I never thought of this – this makes everything easier..." James said...

"It sure does..." Alex said as they put the dresser in the pods. Harland came back first and picked up two dresser drawers, followed by James and Alex. When they were finished, they took the chest and nightstands out the same way...

"Ma – I think you should put this bed in the dumpster..."

"What am I supposed to sleep on?"

"I have a bed in the guest room..."

"That's nice – what am I supposed to sleep on when I move out?"

"You can take the bed from my guest room or I can buy you a new bed..."

"Okay – put it in the dumpster..."

"You got it Ms. Wilkins..." James said...

"Okay Harland – what are you taking?" Alex asked...

"My furniture is going in the dumpster – I'll put the drawers on the bed and the rest can go..."

"Okay – let's do it!" James said. They all had it down and got the bulk of the furniture out the rooms... "How many more rooms we got?" James asked...

"We have one bedroom, the living room, and the dining room table..." Harland answered...

"Harland – if you put the living room furniture in there we won't have anything to sit on..." Helen said...

"True – but I can't move that sectional by myself..."

"Okay – we doin' the living room?" Alex asked...

"Yea..." Harland answered...

"Okay - let's git it!" Alex said as they began moving the living room furniture into the pods. When they were done, they went inside and Harland stood at the entrance to the bedroom...

"You aaight?" James asked...

"Yea..." Harland sighed...

"This was his father's room..." Helen explained...

"He used to always tell us to stay out his room..." Harland sighed...

"Are we moving this to the pods?" Alex asked...

"Yea – I can't get rid of my father's desk..."

"Okay – what about the computer?" James asked...

"That can go in the dumpster..."

"Harland – there's stuff on that computer..."

"Ma – I had that stuff transferred a while back – once it hits the dumpster, whoever wants it is more than welcome to dive in and get it..."

"Okay..." Helen sighed. The guys moved the desk into the pods, came back for the computer, put it in the dumpster, and then they stopped and looked around...

"Shit – it's just 12..." James said...

"You know how we do..." Alex said...

"Thanks guys – I owe you one..."

"Harland – I know you wanted to get the furniture moved out – but you didn't leave anything for us to sit on or sleep on..." Helen said...

"Ma – we have beds to sleep on and furniture to sit on in the condo..."

"Oh – I forgot..."

"Come outside with me and take a look at the garage..." he said as he held the door open for his mother. Helen came out and when she got to the garage, she was stunned...

"Oh my God! I'd forgotten how big this was!"

"Me too..."

"We're gonna be crowded in your condo – you sure you don't mind me being there?"

"Ma – it's only for two weeks..."

"What if it takes longer?"

"C'mon Ma...." he laughed as they went back in the house...

"Hey Ladies!"

"Hey my ass – why haven't we heard from you?" Snow snapped...

"I'm sorry – a lot's been going on..."

"We would've know that if you had told us..." Yyanna said...

"I'm sorry – I'll try not to go too long without talkin' to y'all..."

"Try? Harmony – I know you didn't move in with him!" Snow snapped...

"Snow – I didn't move in with him..."

"Well why haven't we heard from you?" Snow asked...

"I don't have an excuse – I'm sorry..."

"I'll think about accepting your apology..." Yyanna said...

"Well?" Snow asked...

"Okay – so – we went out for happy hour – to celebrate..."

"Aww shit – he proposed?" Snow asked...

"No –he met his realtor at the hotel – he put an offer in on the place for his mother and he put his house on the market..."

"Okay so it's official – he's not just stringing you along – okay..." Snow said...

"I asked him if his mother was going to be there – he said no – we got a table – she shows up..."

"See – why doesn't he check her?" Yyanna asked...

"Okay – I'ma tell y'all – when the waitress came over, I told her this is my mother-in-law..."

"Oh shit!" they exclaimed...

"So she said Harland do you have something you need to tell me? And he says as a matter-of-fact – I do..."

"Oh shit – y'all had her thinking you were engaged!" Snow laughed...

"So she says when's the big day and Harland tells her I just put the house on the market today!" I laughed...

"Yo! I can't!" Snow laughed...

"That's what the fuck she get!" Yyanna laughed...

"She says you just did that without discussing it with me and Harland says Mother – we had a discussion – don't you remember?"

"Oh I know she was mad!" Snow snapped...

"She says you know what – this some bullshit – and she gets up and leaves!" I laughed...

"So what – too bad – fuck her!" Snow snapped...

"I'm with Snow..." Yyanna said...

"So we ate, we drank, he asked me was I comin' over and I told him I wanted to go home – he asked me could he come – I said yea – he asked me could he stay – I said yea..."

"Oh shit! He spent the night?" snow asked...

"Yea..." I sighed...

"Did you get any sleep?" Yyanna asked...

"I got more dick than sleep..." I laughed...

"I know that's right!" Snow laughed...

"He told his mother I was moving in with him after she moved out..."

"Harmony..." Snow started to say...

"I'm not moving in with him – don't worry!" I laughed...

"Harmony – we can't trust you..." Yyanna said...

"Exactly!" Snow acknowledged...

"Okay – can you trust that I can't move in with him with his mother living upstairs?"

"That's true – you have a point..." Yyanna said...

"She has a point and Harland's dick has a head – and right now – Harmony's listening to his head!" Snow laughed...

"I love him..." I sighed...

"What?!"

"He loves me too..."

"See – this is exactly why I said what I said – Harmony's gonna be right there..."

"Snow – I'm not moving in with him..."

"If you say so..." she said as she rolled her eyes...

"I invited him over for dinner yesterday..."

"Did his mother come?" Yyanna asked...

"No she did not – I told him please don't bring her!" I laughed...

"Harmony – le'me ask you a question..." Snow said...

"Okay..."

"Do you see this as a long-term thing?"

"Yea..."

"Okay – le'me ask you another question..."

"Okay..."

"Do you think you'll ever be able to get along with his mother?"

"Yea..."

"Really?" Yyanna asked...

"I think after she gets settled she'll realize he's not trying to cut her out his life..."

"Harmony – she doesn't like you – she's just tolerating you for her son..." Snow said...

"I know..."

"That doesn't bother you?"

"Honestly?"

"Yes – honestly..."

"I wish we got along – but we don't – it is what it is – I love her son –he loves me – we both have to make the best of it..."

"I wish you didn't have to go through that..." Yyanna said...

"I do too – but I love Harland – so I gotta suck it up..."

"Well he gets another point for trying to check his mother..." Snow said...

"He needs to check her 24-7..." Yyanna said...

"Damn – she treats him like he's still her child..." Snow said...

"He called me earlier..."

"Okay..." they both said...

"His mother went off on the guy that put a for sale sign in front of the house..."

"See – that's not right..." Yyanna said...

"That's why he's moving his mother in with him – this way when people want to see the house – she won't be there..."

"When's this happening?" Snow asked...

"He's moving her in today and tomorrow – he's taking her out Saturday so the realtor can show the house..."

"See – she better be glad she's his mother – I'on even know if Flick would put up with this shit!" Snow exclaimed...

"He told me she cried – he felt so bad..."

"Tell him don't fall for that – those are crocodile tears..." Yyanna said...

"I told him to be careful – but I think the best thing I can do is let him find out on his own..."

"I know that's right Harmony!" Snow exclaimed...

"I love him – but I'm not putting up with his mother's shit..."

"Yea right – whatever..." Snow said as she rolled her eyes...

"I'm not!" I laughed...

"Harmony – I hope everything works out..." Yyanna said...

"Me too..."

"Are you going to see him at all this weekend?" Snow asked...

"Hopefully I'll see him Sunday..." I sighed...

"Why you gotta wait 'till Sunday?"

"He said he was taking his mother out on Saturday..."

"So you can't go?" Yyanna asked...

"I didn't say I wanted to go..."

"Stop! Wrong! Hell no!" Snow exclaimed...

"What?" Yyanna and I both said...

"Harmony – that's your man – right?"

"Yea..."

"You wanna see him – right?"

"Yea..."

"Call him and tell him you wanna see him Friday night – matter fact – don't even call him – show up at his house – HIS HOUSE!"

"Okay, okay!" I laughed...

"What if his mother comes?" Yyanna asked...

"She's gonna be there regardless – Harmony – if that's your man – and you want him – go get him!"

"Yes Maam!" I laughed...

"Harmony?"

"Yes Yyanna..."

"Don't make us look for you again..."

"Okay!" Snow exclaimed...

"I won't – I promise..."

I couldn't stop thinking about what Snow said. I wanted to hear his voice. I wanted to see him. I wanted to feel him... "Fuck it..." I said as I got off the train. I ordered an uber, got in, and headed straight to his place. When the uber pulled up, I saw Harland and his mother walking up the steps...

"Harland!" I called out as I got out the uber and closed the door...

"Harmony!" he exclaimed as he hurried over to me, picked me up off the ground, and spun me around...

"I guess you're happy to see me..."

"Very..." he breathed as he kissed me. I could see Helen looking at us and I could also see she was pissed...

"Hi Helen..." I said as Harland took my hand and we went up the steps. Helen followed behind us. When we got inside, I saw a few of the changes... "Oh this is nice!" I exclaimed...

"Thanks..." Harland said...

"Where's the furniture?" I asked...

"You didn't see that pods outside? Helen answered...

"To be honest – I only saw you and Harland..." I answered as I headed towards the bathroom...

"Umm... where are you going?"

"To the bathroom..."

"Well – make sure you stay outta my room..."

"I've already seen it..." I said as I went to pee. When I came out the bathroom, Helen was sitting on the couch and Harland was at the table as I sat down with him... "How's everything going with the house?"

"That's none of your business..." Helen answered...

"We got everything out – it went smooth – thanks to my friends James and Alex..." Harland explained...

"I'm glad – you must be tired...

"Yea... I'm tired..."

"I could give you a massage..."

"Yea?"

"And just where do you think you're going to be massaging him at?" Helen asked...

"Wherever he wants..." I answered as I smiled at Harland mischievously... "Have you had dinner?"

"No – I was just getting ready to order from Thelma's – why don't you stay and have dinner with us?"

"I'd love too..." I sighed. I saw Helen was fuming and I loved it...

"Ma – should I get you your usual?"

"Yes – get me my usual..."

"What can I get you Harmony?"

"Shrimp, yams, and macaroni & cheese..."

"You need some vegetables..." Helen said. Harland shook his head and ordered the food. I wanted to laugh but I knew he was mad so I didn't...

"How was your day Harmony?" he asked...

"Long..." I laughed...

"What do you do for a living?" Helen asked...

"I work in the office of Fair Hearings..."

"You mean you work at DSS..."

"Yes – that's right..."

"You should've just said that..."

"I said what I wanted to say..."

"Umm – so Harmony – how long are you staying?"

"It's Friday night – I can stay as long as you like..."

"Who is it?" Harland asked as somebody knocked at the door...

"It's Charles – your order is here..."

"I'll be right there..." Harland said as he got up and went out into the hallway...

"Harmony – le'me tell you one mutha-fuckin' thing – I'm not going anywhere!" Helen snapped...

"Hmmm – you sure about that? Last I heard you were going to hell..."

"Thanks Charles..." Harland said as he took the bag of food from him...

"You're welcome..."

"Listen – I need you to do me a favor..."

"What can I do for you Mr. Wilkins?"

"Between you and me – I'm buying the unit upstairs for my mother..."

"That's great! Congratulations!"

"Thanks – but please don't tell her..."

"Okay – I'll keep it under my hat..."

"Thanks Charles – I appreciate it..."

"Took you long enough – I'm hungry!" I laughed...

"Thank you Harland..." Helen said as she rolled her eyes. When he took the food out the bag, I saw that they both had chicken wings...

"Oohhh – can I have a chicken wing?"

"If you wanted chicken wings – you should've ordered chicken wings..." Helen said...

"Here..." Harland said as he put one on my plate...

"Thank you Babe – you want some shrimp?"

"Naa – I'm good..."

"Helen – would you like some shrimp?"

"Sure – thank you..." she said as she took a piece. Harland smiled as we ate. When we were finished, Harland got up and cleaned off the table...

"I'm going to get going..." I yawned...

"I thought you were going to stay a while?" Harland asked as his mother smiled...

"I want to – but..."

"You're staying..."

"Okay..."

"I'm going to my room – thanks for dinner..." Helen said as she got up, went in her room, and closed the door...

"Come here..." he commanded as he pulled me into a kiss... "I missed you..."

"I missed you too..."

"Why'd you say you were leaving?"

"I'm tired..."

"I wish you could stay here..."

"Absolutely not..." I laughed...

"My mother goes to sleep early..." he breathed in my ear...

"Harland – No..." I laughed...

"You said you'd give me a massage..."

"I did..."

"So come with me..." he breathed as he kissed me again... "And give me a massage..."

"Harland – No – I'm sorry..." I laughed...

"Ma – I'm taking Harmony home – I'll be back..." he said as he picked up his keys and then we left...

"Okay Bitch – you won this battle... but you won't win the war..."

When we got in the house, Harland was extremely aggressive...

"Harland... wait..."

"No..."

"Harland... stop..."

"No..."

"Harland!" I exclaimed as I pulled away from him. He looked at me with lust in his eyes. I knew I didn't have much time... "I need to get the oils..."

"Oils?" he asked as he inched towards me...

"Yes..." I laughed as I backed away from him but towards the steps...

"What you need to do..." he said as he inched closer and yanked me into his arms... "Is get your ass upstairs...” he said as he slapped my ass...

“Okay!” I laughed as I hurried upstairs with him right behind me... “Harland!”

“What?” he laughed as he pushed me down on the bed...

“I need you to take your clothes off and get on your back...” I said as I got up off the bed...

“I like the sound of that...” he said as he stripped down, got on the bed, and got on his back...

“Okay – I’ll be right back...” I said as I went in the bathroom. Harland heard me opening the drawers and startled me...

“What are you doing?”

“Harland – go lay down on your back like I told you to!”

“Yes Mistress...” he laughed as he went to do as he was told. When I started taking my clothes off, he sat up... “I think I’m going to like this...”

“You will...” I said as I put the oils on the end table and got up on the bed behind his head...

“What are you doing up there?” he laughed...

“Close your eyes... and relax...” I said as I picked up the lotion containing camphor, menthol, clove, and eucalyptus, put some in my hands, and began massaging his shoulders...

“Mmmm... that feels nice...” he breathed. I added some more lotion, picked up his head, opened my legs around his head and massaged his upper arms… "Oohhh… yeesss…" he breathed. I applied some more lotion to my hands and when I bent over to massage his lower arms, my pussy was touching his forehead…

"You ain't right…" he laughed…

"Let me finish…" I laughed…

"As soon as you let go of my arms… I'm going to punish you…"

"I'm looking forward to it…" I said as I applied some more lotion to my hands, straddled his chest below his chin so he couldn't reach my pussy, and began massaging his upper thighs…

"Okay… let's play…" he said as he applied some lotion to his hands and began massaging my ass… "How does this feel?"

"You tell me…" I answered as I applied some more lotion to my hands, moved my pussy down right above his dick, bent over, and began massaging his lover legs…

"You know you wrong…" he laughed. I moved my hands from his lower legs and began massaging his left foot… "Ooohhh…" he moaned. I massaged his foot completely with both hands and then I began massaging each toe… "That tickles…" I moved over to the right foot and repeated the same technique as he moaned… "Ooohhh…" When I was done, I crawled down his body because I knew he'd grab me and tongue my pussy down if I want back the same way I came… "Come here…" he commanded…

"Not yet..." Harland smiled at me and anticipated what was going to happen next... "Get on your stomach..."

"Okay..." he said as he flipped over. I straddled him across his back, applied lotion to my hands, and began massaging his upper back...

"Ooohhh... that feels good..." I massaged him until I felt his muscles relax and then I applied some more lotion to my hands and moved to his lower back... "Uuuggghhh..." he moaned. As I massaged his lower back, I could tell he was carrying a lot. It took a while for his lower back to loosen up and when it finally did, I applied some more lotion to my hands, moved myself down to his ass, and planted kisses all over it as I massaged each cheek... "Ooohhh..." he moaned. I applied more lotion to my hands and began massaging his upper thighs as I planted more kisses on the bottom of his ass. I was expecting him to tense up but he didn't, so I applied more lotion to my hands, and massaged his lower legs... "Ooohhh..." he moaned. When I was done, I got up off him and stood up... "What now Mistress?" he asked as he turned over...

"I'm going to get on the bed on my knees..."

"Okay..."

"I'm going to sit on the back of my legs and face the headboard..."

"Okay..."

"I'm going to hold on to the headboard as you ease yourself inside me..."

"Oh... okay..."

"Once you're inside me, you're going to apply some lotion to your hands, and massage me from the inside to the outside..." I explained as I got on the bed, sat back on my legs, leaned forward, and grabbed the headboard. Harland applied some lotion to his hands, held on to my shoulders, and eased himself inside me... "Oohhh... Harland..." I moaned. He moved slowly and massaged my shoulders and my back... "Huh... Harland..." I moaned. He applied more lotion to his hands and began massaging my breasts... "Oohhh... Harland..." I moaned. He applied more lotion, moved down to my stomach, and massaged my stomach and my hips as he began thrusting a little faster... "Ohh Harland... Yesss..." Harland grabbed my hips and picked up the pace as I began bouncing on his dick... "Harland... Fuck... I'm cumming..."

"Cum for me..." he breathed in my ear...

"Haah... Haah... Haah... Haah... Hhhaaahhh!!"

"Huh... Huh... Huh... Huh... Hhhuuuhhh!!"

"Oh Harland..." I breathed...

"Get on your back..." he commanded. I did as I was told and Harland was back inside me again as we were kissing and sensually sucking each other's tongues... "Shit..." he breathed as his phone rang. I looked over at his phone, saw it was his mother, and answered it...

"H... Hello... Helen..."

"Put Harland on the phone..."

"He's... busy... he'll... call... you... back..." I breathed before I hung up...

"I can't... believe... you... just... did... that..." he breathed as he put his arms up under my back and fucked me deeper...

"Good morning!" Helen exclaimed...

"Good morning..."

"Where are we going today?"

"Where would you like to go Ma?"

"I'd like to go to Milford Mall, Cracker Barrel, the movies...

"What would you like to do first?"

"Doesn't matter..."

"Okay then – we'll go to Cracker Barrel for breakfast, then we'll go to the mall – and we'll go to the movies if you're not too tired..."

"Me? Tired? Aahhh haaa!" she laughed as they left...

"Damn I wish you were still here..." I sighed as I ran my hands up and down my naked body... "As soon as your mother gets the fuck out

– I can move the fuck in – and I will fuck you... and suck you... Le'me get up!" I laughed as I got up and went to the bathroom. "I'm going to take a shower, get dressed, and go buy my man a gift – maybe I'll go to Milford today – who knows?"

"Will there be anything else?" the waitress asked...

"No thank you..." Harland answered...

"Nothing else for me..." Helen answered...

"Here's your check – you can pay on your way out..." the waitress said as she walked away...

"I'm sure gonna miss this..." Helen sighed...

"Miss what Ma?"

"This – you and me - spending the day together..."

"Ma – stop it..."

"I'm just saying – you're going to be with Harmony a lot more now that she's moving in..."

"Yes Ma – I will be with Harmony a lot more – but that doesn't mean I won't be spending any time with you..."

"She couldn't even let us have the weekend – she didn't have to come over yesterday – I barely got moved in and here she is all up in my face..."

"Let's go..." he said as he got up...

"Are we still going to the mall?"

"Yes Ma..." he sighed...

"Are you mad at me?"

"I'm about to be if you don't come on..." he lied. I told him I wasn't moving in but deep down, I knew he really wanted me to...

"I'm going to go to this cute lil' key shop in the Milford Mall and get a key made for my man!" I exclaimed as the uber pulled up...

"Harland – how's this?" Helen asked as she came out the dressing room..."

"Wow!" Harland exclaimed...

"I know – right?" she gushed...

"I haven't seen you this happy since..."

"Since your father..."

"Yea..."

"I still got it..." she said as she spun around..."

"Yea Ma – you still got it..." he agreed as she went back into the dressing room...

"How can I help you?" he associate asked...

"I'd like to duplicate this key..." I answered as I gave him my key...

"We have this in stock – would you like any particular color?"

"Yes – I'd like that metallic blue..."

"Yes Maam..." he said as he went to make my duplicate key...

"Hello Sheddi..."

"Harland – we have an offer – full asking..."

"Oh my God!"

"So I have to tell you a couple of things..."

"Okay..."

"He has an FHA pre-approval..."

"What's that?"

"FHA is federally funded – so it has to pass inspection and the house has to appraise for the asking price...

"I'm not worried about the inspection – but what if it doesn't appraise for full asking?"

"The worst thing that can happen is that it doesn't pass inspection – as long as it passes inspection, if they feel the house is over-priced, you'll have to lower the asking or accept their appraisal..."

"What if I don't accept their appraisal?"

"You won't have too – but if you try to sell it to anyone else that has financing, the appraisal is on record..."

"Okay – I'll take the money and run!" he laughed...

"I did a comparison in the neighborhood – I don't think you'll have anything to worry about – in the meantime, I'm going to forward you the offer – can you print it out, sign it, and get it back to me?"

"Here's your keys..." the associate said as he handed them to me...

"Thank you..."

"Would you like anything else?"

"I'd like that gift box..."

"Would you like me to put your new key in the box for you?"

"Yes please..."

"Okay..." I gave him the metallic blue key, he put it in the box, tied a red ribbon around it, and handed it to me...

"Thank you!" I exclaimed as I put the box in my pocket, hurried out the shop, and ran right into Harland...

"Hey!" he laughed as I ran into him...

"Hi!" I exclaimed as I pulled him into a kiss and kissed him hard...

"What are you doing here?"

"Here!" I exclaimed as I gave him the box...

"For me?"

"Yes – open it!" I exclaimed as Helen walked up...

"Hello..."

"Hi Helen..."

"Harmony – you're giving me a key? To your house?"

"Yea..."

"Why does he need a key to your house if you're moving in with him?" Helen asked...

"Thank you..." he breathed as he kissed me...

"You're welcome..." Helen was seething...

"Harland – I'm ready to go to the movies..." she sighed...

"We will – but while you were in there Sheddi called – I got an offer..."

"Harland – that's great!" I exclaimed as we hugged...

"How much?" Helen asked...

"We'll talk about that later – right now I need to go to Fed Ex – I need to print out this offer, sign it, date it, and send it back to Sheddi..."

"Okay..." I said as I got up to go with them...

"Harland – I thought we were going to the movies?" Helen asked as if she didn't hear what he just said...

"We are – I just need to take care of this first..." he said as we all went towards Fed Ex... "Wait here – this will only take a few minutes..." he said and then he went over to one of the printing stations. Helen got up, went over to the printing station, and stood behind him as he printed everything out. The pages printed out quickly so she wasn't able to read them... "Ma – go sit back down – I'll be done in a minute..." he said as he scanned over the papers, found the signature lines, signed them, dated them, and put them on the scanner...

"Let me see that!" she snapped as she tried to take the paper off the scanner and Harland stopped her...

"Ma – No!"

"Why not?"

"You know what – forget it – we don't need to go to the movies – we can just go home..."

"I'll be over there with Harmony..." she sighed as she came back to sit with me. Harland finished scanning the documents and put them in the shredder. When he was finished, he came over to us... "Where's the papers?"

"I shredded them..."

"Why would you do that?"

"I already have them scanned to my email – I don't need to carry personal papers in my pocket..." The truth was his mother was trying to get her hands on those papers..." and he knew it...

"Harmony – we're going to the movies – you comin'?" he asked me. We could both see that Helen was pissed...

"Sure..." I answered...

"Anything in particular you wanna see?" he asked...

""I'd like to see The Photograph..." Helen answered...

"So would I!" I exclaimed...

"Let's go..." Harland said as Helen took one arm and I took the other arm. When the movie was over, we all went to the car and I laughed to myself as she ran to get in the front seat. To me, that was so trivial. I knew I was a priority in Harland's life, so it didn't matter where I sat in the car...

"We're home..." Harland said as we pulled up. I didn't wait for him to open the door for me – I got out and stretched... "C'mon..." Harland said as we followed him into the building...

"Hello Mr. Wilkins..." Charles greeted...

"Hello Charles – could you let us in Unit 2J?"

"I sure can..." he smiled as he got in the elevator with us. Helen looked back and forth between the two of us as we smiled. When we got off the elevator, Charles opened the door for us, and we went inside...

"What's this?" Helen asked...

"This is your new home..." Harland answered...

"This is a joke – right?"

"Umm... No... this isn't a joke..." Harland answered...

"Let me help you understand something..." Helen said as she went over to the window... "You put me out my house – you sell my house out from under me – and you think I'm going to be happy here?!"

"Actually – yes – I thought you'd be happy here..."

"Why the fuck would I be happy living in an apartment when I had my own house?"

"Ma – it was time to let that go!"

"So you say! You never asked me how I felt!"

"I didn't need to ask you how you felt – you made it perfectly clear that you wanted me to continue taking care of you and continue paying all the bills in the house...”

“I brought you into this world – it’s the least you can do...”

“Ma – I’m not your husband – I’m not your man – I’m your son!”

“See – you let this Bitch control you – you’re so knee-deep in her pussy you’ve lost your got-damned mind!”

“You know what – I’m out...” I said as I started to leave and Harland stopped me...

“Don’t leave – please...” he asked as he took my hand... “First of all – I don’t owe you anything – I did all that for you because I love you – second – you owe Harmony an apology for calling her out her name and disrespecting her...”

“Oh please – I call it as I see it – don’t try to turn this on me – you got at least $340k for my house – you owe me $170k – and I’ma need you to run me my money so I can buy myself a house – not an apartment!”

“First of all – you never paid a dime on that house – Dad paid the mortgage up until he left – before he left you, he left the house to me – I paid the mortgage until the house was paid off – I paid the heat, water, sewer, electric – I’ve been paying the taxes – and I bought you this condo - all you ever did was buy food, clothes, and weaves – so basically, I don’t owe you a got-damned thing!”

"Well – you're gonna need to use that key Harmony gave you to her house – she won't be moving in because I'm not moving out – and you can sell this condo for all I care 'cause I'm not moving until you put me in a house!"

"Ma – I'm done – as soon as we close, I'm moving your things up here... I'm giving you your keys..." and what you do after that is your business..." he said as he opened the door to leave...

"So that's it? You're done?" Harland took my hand and led me out the door...

"Aaaggghhh!" he boomed as he punched the wall. I didn't say anything. I knew he was angry and hurt. As much as I couldn't stand her, I'd rather he hit the wall then hit his mother... "I should 'a put her ass in a fuckin' senior citizen complex! Fuckin' ungrateful Bitch!" he yelled as he threw his kitchen table over and broke it... "Great – just what the fuck I need!" he yelled as he picked up a chair and threw it across the living room...

"Mr. Wilkins – it's Charles – open the door!"

"What?!" Harland snapped as he snatched the door open...

"You alright?" he asked me...

"I'm fine..."

"Charles – I'd never hurt her..."

"How was I supposed to know that – oh shit – you need me to help you clean that up?"

"Charles – thank you – I'm alright – I got it..."

"I've never seen you like this – what happened?"

"Long story..." he sighed... "Is my mother still upstairs?"

"Your mother left..."

"Okay – thanks..."

"You're welcome..."

"Charles – if you don't mind..."

"Oh sure – if you need anything – I'm outside..." he said as Harland closed the door in his face. I got up, went over to him, pulled him into a hug, and he broke down...

"I tried..."

"Come here..." I said as I took his hand and led him to the couch...

"I did the best I could..."

"I know..."

"She's never satisfied..."

"I know..."

"Please don't leave me..."

"Never..."

"I can't wait until this is over – I wish I could move her things up there today..."

"Why can't you?"

"We haven't closed yet..."

"So what?"

"So basically, I'd be breaking the law..."

"Who's gonna tell?"

"I don't wanna risk it..."

"Call Sheddi – ask her to ask the seller if your mother can move in..."

"What if they say no?"

"What if they say yes?"

"I'll call her now..." he said as he took out his phone and called...

"Harland – I received your contract – we might be able to close next week so you can do both at the same time..."

"Sheddi – is it possible my mother can move in before the closing?"

"All's not well in paradise?"

"Yea..."

"I can ask – I'll get back to you in a few minutes..."

"Thank you Sheddi..."

"You want something to drink?" he asked...

"Sure..."

"You want some wine?"

"Naa – I'll have a Guinness..."

"Coming right up..." he said as he opened the fridge, took out two bottles, opened them, and handed one to me...

"To us..." I said...

"To us..." he said as his phone rang...

"Hello Sheddi..." he answered as he put the phone on speaker...

"Harland – I spoke with the realtor..."

"Okay..."

"Since you offered full asking and you waived the inspection, the seller is okay with your mother moving in before closing..."

"Thank you Sheddi..."

"You're welcome – I'll see you next week..."

"Thank you Lord!" he exclaimed...

"Thank you Lord!" I exclaimed as we finished our beers...

"Charles!" Harland yelled as he went out into the hallway...

"What's wrong?" Charles asked as he hurried over...

"I need to take you up on your offer..."

"Sure – what do you need me to do?'

"You see that pods out there?"

"Oh shit – are you serious?"

"I'm afraid so..."

"C'mon..." Charles laughed as he went to help Harland move everything out the pods...

Excerpt from Harmony

"Excuse me – Ms. Wilkins..." Charles said as he tried to get Helen's attention...

"I'm in a hurry..." she barked...

"Yes Maam – I can see that – Mr. Wilkins wanted me to give you these..." he said as he took the keys out his pocket and gave them to her...

"Thanks – but I already have keys..."

"Ms. Wilkins – those are the keys to your place..."

"My place?"

"Yes Maam – you live in Unit 2J – right?"

"Hell no I don't live up there!"

"Ms. Wilkins – I'm sorry – I helped Mr. Wilkins move all of your things upstairs while you were gone yesterday..."

"What?!"

"Yes Maam – all your things are in your place... and I was told to give you the keys as soon as I saw you..."

"We'll see about this!" she snapped as she got on the elevator... "Mutha fucka think he can just put me out like this – fuck him..." she said as she went inside... "Well, well... what do we have here?" she asked as she looked on the sectional and saw the gift box I have him... "Harland – you probably don't even realize you lost your key to her house... Hmmm... I'll get this right back to you – I just need to make a copy for myself first..." she said as she put the box in her pocket and went out the door...